INTERGALACTIC BABYSITTER ORIENTATION GUIDE

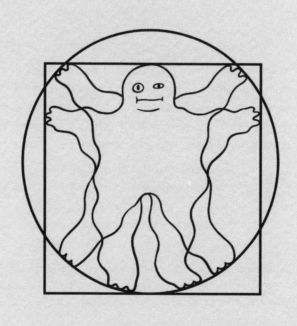

Art by Devin Taylor

Design by Lindsay Broderick

Printed in the United States of America

First Hardcover Edition, May 2020

FAC-038091-20101

ISBN 978-1-368-05359-4

Library of Congress Control Number: 2019944672

For more Disney Press fun, visit www.disneybooks.com

Visit DisneyChannel.com

SUSTAINABLE FORESTRY INITIATIVE Certified Sourcing
www.sfiprogram.org
SFI-00993

Logo Applies to Text Stock Only

DISNEP
GABBY DURAN
& THE UNSITTABLES

INTERGALACTIC
BABYSITTER
ORIENTATION GUIDE

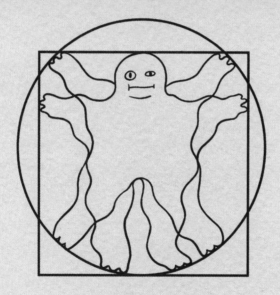

BY CARIN DAVIS

BASED ON THE SERIES CREATED BY
MIKE ALBER AND GABE SNYDER

DISNEP PRESS

LOS ANGELES ● NEW YORK

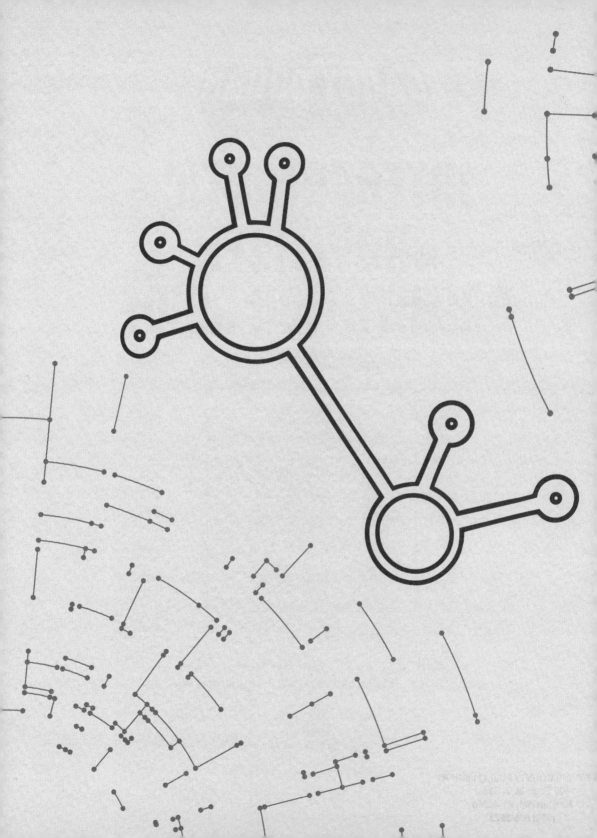

Hi! Gabby Duran here. I'm the best babysitter in all of ~~Havensburg~~ ~~the world~~ the galaxy. Anybody can babysit their younger brother or sister. (I'm not saying it's easy. I've spent plenty of challenging nights looking after my sister, Olivia. Like the night she got chocolate cake all over the couch. Okay, fine, technically I was the one who ate the double-chocolate-crunch cupcake on the couch and left crumbs all over the cushions. But in my defense, it happened while I was babysitting Olivia. So it's basically the same thing.)

Anyways, my point is that lots of middle schoolers babysit their sibs, their cousins, or their next-door neighbors. That's standard-issue tween responsibility right there. But me? I babysit aliens.

You heard me. Aliens. From another planet. As in not Earthlings. How dope is that? I'm talking about legit from outer space, extraterrestrial kids I'm in charge of watching. And you know what? I pretty much rule at it. Oh, who am I kidding? I definitely rule at it. Which is why I'm here to share a few tips. When it comes to babysitting unsittables, I'm your expert. When it comes to eating tacos and taquitos, I'm also your expert. I set the town's all-time taco-eating record at the Luchachos Taco Takedown.

my picture's even up in the taqueria. That's where you might recognize me from. But that's a whole different skill set. I can't possibly teach you how to become a taco champion. You're either born with it, or you're not. But babysitting? There's a thing or two you can learn from me there.

This binder contains the top-secret, all-important official <u>Intergalactic Babysitter Orientation Guide.</u> Principal Principal Swift (that's his real name, not kidding) gave it to me before I started watching his nephew, Jeremy. He said I was required to read every word of it before my first alien-sitting gig. So what did I do? Threw it in the garbage can. Never read a word of it. Which, looking back, may have been a mistake. I should have read it. And I will read it . . . someday. It's just, the orientation materials contain so. Many. Rules. Like seventy-eight rules. It's basically just a long, boring binder of instructions. I've checked out a couple of them during major panic situations, and I'll admit, they've come in handy. But let's be honest, I'm not really down with rules. I'm more of a wing-it-in-the-moment kinda girl.

Anyways, the official orientation materials are here, along with a few other tips and tricks I've picked up on my babysitting adventures. So you're all set. Babysitting is, without a doubt, the best job in the universe. And if you're worried about messing up, don't be. You got this! Just remember, if you're babysitting a kid who won't stop crying no matter what you do, it could always be worse. She could be crying out of all nine of her mouths.

Later,

The One and Only

Gabby Duran

Greetings, Gabby Duran.

It is I. Principal Principal Swift here. The bloke who put the "prince" in principal. And the "pal" in principal. I put them both in there. Righty-hoo then, anyways . . .

The official *Intergalactic Babysitter Orientation Guide* that follows will provide you instruction on the unbreakable rules and regulations of extraterrestrial child watching. I'm sure you'll find the material both informative and interesting, and that you'll read it with the utmost thoroughness. *ummmmm. If thinking that makes you happy, then sure. Who am I to crush your dreams?*

Let's get started then, shall we?

Now that you are aware that aliens live right here in Havensburg, you are most likely filled with Earthling curiosity. Let me answer a few of the more pressing questions that may be filling your mind as you embark on your babysitting journey.

Why are aliens here?

The answer to that question is complicated. Every alien family has their own specific reason for residing on Earth. Some alien families fled their war-torn planets in search of a more peaceful upbringing for their children. Others racked up enough constant cosmic flier miles to earn a free business-class ticket to Earth and are, thus, merely here on vacation. One family moved here when their dad was granted a job studying classic Earthling literature at a prominent university. One family just really likes to eat the Earthling delicacy that goes by the name cotton candy. *I can respect that.*

Then you have the case of my nephew, Jeremy, who is set to be the next supreme leader on the planet Gor-Monia. But there are those on our planet who would be quite happy to see him fail to ascend to this role. Jeremy and I are to stay here on Earth until he comes of governing age. It was also of the utmost importance that we separate him from his sister, Dranis. The bickering between those two could drive a blob mad.

Why do aliens need a babysitter? Aren't they here with their parents?

Oh, Gabby. Gabby, Gabby, Gabby, Gabby. The Gabster. Gabbity Gabs Gab. The answers to those questions are as varied as the stars. Alien parents must temporarily take leave of their children for a variety of vital reasons: to attend to pressing duties at their human workplace, to partake in the everyday human social pursuit called town gossip, or to complete the emergency binge-watching of *The Real Blob-Wives of Gor-Monia*, season forty-three. You would not believe what happens next on that program. Oh, I love it so. *Obviously, I have so many questions. . . .*

Additional reasons you may be asked to sit? A little thing called the bucket list. I, for one, shall be doing much crossing off of it. There are hills to climb, dinner parties to crash, chickens to ask why they're crossing the road. *Okay, yeah, I'm just gonna leave that one there for now.*

And let us not forget attending popular events where human adults go to nap, like the symphony. Am I correct in that thinking? I've also heard that visiting an Earthling dentist is a unique adventure. Personally, I cannot wait to experience the thrill of such an excursion and will require a sitter for that. And the final reason for a babysitter? Sometimes even alien parents just need a night off.

As our Earthly presence must be kept a secret, it is necessary for this supervision to take place in the home. Alien youth simply don't possess the wherewithal to participate in human society without revealing that they're you-know-what. The risk is simply too high. So when alien parents are scheduled to be otherwise occupied, they cannot follow the example of their human counterparts and simply drop their children off at elementary school, keep them busy at youth soccer practice, or have them attend rehearsals for those at best mediocre school choir assemblies the music teacher is always blabbing about. No, no, no. Therefore, the only solution to be had is one where a human babysitter watches over the alien children in the family home.

And that, my friends, is where I come in.

What's your mission?

As the one and only sanctioned alien sitter in the municipality of Havensburg, your mission is to protect the safety and well-being of our next generation of aliens, to guard the secret of our alien presence with the utmost discretion, and to help us blend in seamlessly with Earth culture. *I got this. Those alien kids won't know what hit 'em when I roll in.*

Is Principal Swift's real last name Hemsworth? *Hold up, WHAT?!*

Oh, yes. Truly a question for the ages. I wish I could answer that. I do. But you don't currently possess a high enough clearance to obtain that information. Perhaps someday you will earn the right to know such a secret. . . .

Cheerio,

PPS

PPS

POTENTIAL BABYSITTERS

REQUIRED QUALITIES OF AN EARTHLING BABYSITTER

- ☐ Organized
- ☐ Responsible
- ☐ Punctual
- ☐ Positive
- ☐ Detail oriented
- ☐ Able to follow directions
- ☐ Trustworthy
- ☐ Patient
- ☐ Safety conscious
- ☐ Nurturing
- ☐ Possessed of sound judgment
- ☐ FEARLESS
- ☐ RESOURCEFUL
- ☐ WILLING TO PROTECT ONE'S CAR FROM BIRD DROPPINGS
- ☐ Able to blow people's minds when they tear up the dance floor

To: Gor-Monite Central Archive
CC: Glor-Bron
From: Principal Principal Swift
Subject: Dossier of Potential Earthling Babysitters in Havensburg
Priority: Alpha

OFFICIAL REPORT

Dear Glor-Bron,

At long last, after careful observation and drawn-out, tedious research (which I found extremely boring), attached please find my report on potential Earthling babysitters. As discussed, the purpose of these files is to identify a suitable human to supervise my nephew, Jeremy, while I complete the tasks required of me as school principal at Havensburg Junior High School, United States, Planet Earth. It's a very important job, you know. I also need someone to watch over Jeremy while I try to assimilate with human culture. I am quite busy participating in exotic Earth activities like meeting people for coffee, dropping off my dry cleaning, and running to the store. I find the last to be the most difficult. It is not easy to jog while carrying reusable shopping bags. I've tried it and always seem to fail. Please see last week's report for more details on this challenging Earthling sport that I plan to conquer.

In conclusion, after reviewing all the potential candidates, I believe the best human for the position is a new student named Gabby Duran. *Oh, yeah. Game recognizes game.*

Gor-bye,

PRINCIPAL PRINCIPAL SWIFT
Principal Principal Swift

Name: Gabby Duran

Age: 13

Family members: Mom—Dina, on-air reporter at Local 6; sister—Olivia, age 8; dad—Bruce, lives in Miami

Known associates: Best friend Wesley

Interests: Horror movies, punk bands, moping around about moving from Miami

Favorite food: Taquitos

Babysitting experience: Babysitting her younger sister, Olivia

Babysitting style: Tenacious. No matter how disastrous the situation, Gabby Duran is not one to give up. She displays remarkable poise and ingenuity in emergency situations. Her ability to act, rather than panic, is notable. Also, she seems to throw herself into the activities in which she is interested, giving her all.

Observations: To borrow an Earthling phrase, Gabby Duran zigs when others might zag. And while on Gor-Monia "zigging" may refer to an illegal act involving chewing bubble gum, which we all know should be avoided at all costs, in this particular case, the Earthling word "zigging" refers to doing things one's own way and thinking on one's feet. Of which, by the way, Gabby only has two.

Thanks, Swifty. That's pretty much the nicest thing anyone's ever said about me. I like you, too, you sweet weirdo.

Name: Susie Glover

Age: 13

Family members: Not available

Known associates: No known friends

Interests: Earning five-star online babysitting reviews, dominating Math Smackdowns

Favorite food: Goji berries, celery jerky, and anything from the health food store

Babysitting experience: Been in the b-sit business for years. (FYI, b-sit is how experienced Earthling childcare professionals refer to babysitting. I think I sound rather cool saying it, don't you?) Anyhoo, Susie has an impressive number of babysitting clients, including all three of the Havensburg Rogers. Yes, all three: Roger Nelson, Roger Daniels, and Roger M. Rogers. As Earthlings say, "Roger that. . . ."

Babysitting style: Susie takes her babysitting responsibilities to an extreme. While professional, her approach to sitting may be too intense for Jeremy. She will stop at nothing to receive a good review, sometimes putting her own reputation before her ward's amusement.

Susie's flawless babysitting vibe? It's off-putting.

Also, she seems a bit, well, uncool. And I can't have the future supreme leader of Gor-Monia following in her uncool footsteps. I should think not, Glor-Bron. I should think not.

Observations: I do commend Susie on the wearing of her self-made Sue-tility belt. I was previously unaware of this high-style Earthling trend and plan to incorporate this fine fashion-forward accessory into my own dapper Earth wardrobe.

Name: Wesley

Age: 13

Family members: Mom, dad, and deceased dog, Brisket.

Known associates: Gabby Duran

Interests: Conspiracy theories, the Illuminati, and anything involving the paranormal. He also loves horror films, in particular the Blooderella movie franchise.

Favorite food: Trail mix

Babysitting experience: As founder of the Mysteries of Havensburg Club, Wesley knows more about aliens and the paranormal than anyone else in Havensburg. However, he has no actual babysitting experience, per se. Wesley wouldn't know how to change a diaper to save his life. And when babysitting aliens, diaper-changing can become a life-or-death situation.

Babysitting style: Inquisitive. Wesley is curious about all things alien and supernatural, and quite welcoming to species of every shape, size, and origin. As such, he would be more likely to befriend an alien than to act as an authority figure to one.

Observations: Wesley does not appear to be a very good secret keeper. He does not demonstrate the necessary discretion required to babysit children from another planet. His motivation lies in finding and exposing alien life in Havensburg. And we simply cannot tolerate that.

Also, he seems to be quite irresponsible, as my research has uncovered. Six years ago, he borrowed *Hopi: A Story of Desert Gardeners* from the Havensburg Public Library and committed the heinous crime of never returning it. The horror! That type of flagrant delinquency is unacceptable for a potential alien sitter. I do believe the gardeners of the desert deserve more respect.

I get it. It's hard to find someone to trust. But Wesley's one of the best, most trustworthy humans there is. Besides, it's pretty sweet to have someone to share this whole babysitting aliens thing with. And who loves aliens more than Wesley?

No one, that's who.

Name: Olivia Duran

Age: 8

Family members: Mom—Dina, on-air reporter at Local 6; sister—Gabby, age 13; dad—Bruce, lives in Miami

Known associates: Gabby Duran, Wesley, various brainiac children from the gifted program

Interests: Havensburg Elementary School Gifted Program, chore wheels, dribbling an Invisi-ball

Favorite food: Sugar-Frosted Blammo Bombs, grilled cheese, Krispy Pops

Babysitting experience: Has spent a lot of time being babysat by her sister, Gabby. Does that count?

Babysitting style: Olivia is quite meticulous about her education and would most likely approach babysitting aliens in the same fastidious way. However, currently, she is simply too young for such an enormous task.

If you're worried about Olivia's age, don't be. My sis is wise beyond her years. Honestly, Swifty, she's wise beyond your years. Come to think of it, I have no idea how old you are. Are you like twenty-five or two hundred and five? Hard to tell . . . might be all the bow ties.

Observations: Olivia appears to be on the higher spectrum of human intelligence. She has won many prestigious awards, including Student of the Month and trophies in English and karate. She also won the class spelling bee. Please note: I am yet unclear why Earthlings award their best spellers a buzzing bee. But I intend to find out and include it in my next report. Perhaps it is because humans of a high intelligence know how to avoid being stung by the little buzzing buggers. I myself have endured the sting of a bee five times since arriving on this planet, which is why I have now taken to practicing my Earthling spelling daily.

Name: Jace

Age: 12

Family members: Not available

Known associates: Too many Big Buddies to name

Interests: Saving the whales, performing charity work in Africa

Favorite food: Yum-yums in his tum-tum, hot dogs loaded with onions

Babysitting experience: Mentoring youth through the Big Buddies program

Babysitting style: Jace takes an active, hands-on approach to his youth volunteer activities. He often entertains his wards with field days, three-legged races, and go-karts.

Observations: Jace appears to be an altruistic young man who gives his time freely to humanitarian and philanthropic causes. He also appears to be what the Earthlings call "dreamy." However, outside of the Hemsworth brothers, I do not trust Earthlings who possess both internal and external perfection. It's annoying.

For the record, my crush on Jace has been crushed. I can't believe I actually liked him. How can one guy care that much about helping displaced potato farmers in Quebec?

Name: Julius

Age: 23

Family members: Not available

Known associates: Lucille, owner of Luchachos, and grandmother Mamá Chaco, who makes a very delicious Earthling meat dish known as carnitas

Interests: Mexican food

Favorite food: Tamales

Babysitting experience: None

Babysitting style: As a waiter at Luchachos Taqueria, Julius has served many kids, tweens, and families with a smile. He has also perfected the art of Earthling small talk. I do believe he could transfer these skills to situations outside of the taqueria environment, but I have not yet collected the required data to prove this theory.

Observations: Julius already has full-time employment at Luchachos and therefore would not be available to babysit aliens on the regular. Also, he is used to receiving a 15 percent tip on top of his set salary, and I do not intend to tip the babysitter. This Earthling behavior of not adding a tip is also known as "being cheap," and mastering it will allow me to blend in seamlessly with some humans.

Turns out Wesley and I are the champions of bad tippers. But we're working on it, Julius. We're working on it.

Name: Vice Principal Klipper

Age: Adult

Family members: Not available, though rumor has it she's engaged to the owner of Swirl Town

Known associates: Not available

Interests: Vice Principal Klipper would very much like to engage in the building of a Chill Room, where students can meditate and find their inner truth. I was unaware that youths are losing their inner truth, and suggest the students search the school's lost and found first. I myself go shopping there, and it is a treasure trove. I have collected quite a few single mittens, a slightly dented superhero lunch box, and an ancient Earthling relic called a mixed tape.

Favorite food: Vice Principal Klipper loves Swirl Town frozen yogurt, otherwise known as froyo in Earthling slang. Apparently, it takes a great deal more effort for humans to utter two syllables than one. Therefore, humans often shorten their words to a single syllable to avoid the tremendous pain and suffering they must endure from speaking in complete words. So froyo it is.

Babysitting experience: Nine years as a teacher and school administrator

Babysitting style: Vice Principal Klipper approaches her in-school interactions with students in a friendly and open style. She would most likely approach babysitting with the same chipper attitude and genuine concern for children's well-being.

Observations: Not only does Vice Principal Klipper want the best for her students, but she also has the best taste in Earthling frozen desserts. She often hands out Swirl Town gift cards just because. A gift card is a small plastic rectangle that an Earthling can trade in at any time for a single froyo cone. You can also simply eat the gift card itself. It makes for quite a crunchy snack. But it's harder to cover in toppings like sprinkles and hot fudge. Believe me, I have tried.

As for Vice Principal Klipper, while she would make an exceptional babysitter, she simply cannot learn my true Gor-Monite identity. It would be a conflict of interest. Unfortunately, this disqualifies her from consideration.

Klipper's whole gift card thing kinda creeps me out. And the way she knows every student's name? It's unnatural. Glad you didn't go with her. And for the record, you are a way better principal than her. Like a million light-years better. Just thought you should know.

Name: Howard

Age: 13

Family members: Not available

Known associates: Not available

Favorite food: Locker hoagie

Babysitting experience: Babysits his younger brother

Babysitting style: Howard tends to taunt and torment those around him. This includes his fellow students, his basketball teammates, and even his teachers. When it comes to athletics, he likes to showboat in a demoralizing fashion.

Observations: Howard is, to use human vernacular, a total ball hog on the court. Using the theory of transference, I conclude he would have difficulty sharing toys with any alien child he watched, as well. He would also not permit the children he's watching to win at a game of checkers, cards, or thumb wrestling. So with regard to his potential as a babysitter, as the Earthlings say, "hard pass."

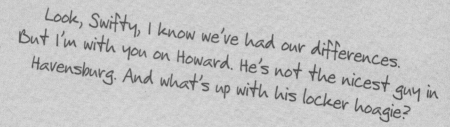

Look, Swifty, I know we've had our differences. But I'm with you on Howard. He's not the nicest guy in Havensburg. And what's up with his locker hoagie?

Name: Mrs. Trenchbock

Age: Old . . . really old

Family members: No one

Known associates: No associates

Interests: Vacationing on singles cruises

Favorite food: Big fan of the buffet

Babysitting style: It is safe to say her approach to watching children is quite traditional in theory and in practice.

Babysitting experience: She has years of experience, maybe centuries, given how old she seems.

Observations: Mrs. Trenchbock smells like funerals and sadness. There are several alien species who like to bottle the smell of sadness and wear it as perfume. So for those species, perhaps Mrs. Trenchbock makes for an excellent supervisorial candidate. However, Gor-Monites are not one of those species. We prefer to wear more playful fragrances, like the intoxicating aroma of durian.

Regardless of her perfume preference, Mrs. Trenchbock likes to, as humans say, kick it old school. And while Gor-Monites do their best to respect their elders, I do not believe Mrs. Trenchbock is the best choice to keep up with Jeremy's feisty energy and youthful temperament.

PRACTICAL TIPS FOR BABYSITTING ALIENS

BABYSITTING GOALS RECOGNIZED ACROSS THE UNIVERSE

Keep the kids safe.

Eh, as long as you return them in one piece, it's all gravy.

Be responsible. The best time to prepare for an event is before it happens.

Where's the fun in that?

Be reliable.

My clients can always 100 percent rely on me . . . being late.

Help teach kids the difference between right and wrong.

Isn't that more of a personal opinion? It's at least a sliding scale. Who's with me on that?

Practice creative discipline.

Who called the fun police?

Safeguard aliens' secret presence on other planets.

Your top-secret alien stuff is safe with me. Since I started, I haven't told anyone about your existence. Except I told Wesley. Actually, Wesley and Olivia—that's it.

Start saving money for college. Just those two. For now.

If by "saving money for college" you mean spending all your earnings on tacos, I'm way ahead of you.

Learn to solve problems strategically.

I have a strategy. Act first, think later.

Encourage kids to stay true to themselves, even when they feel like outsiders. Nailed it.

QUIZ: ARE YOU READY TO BABYSIT AN ALIEN?

Think you've got what it takes to babysit children from another galaxy? Test your knowledge on our Intergalactic Sitter Skillz Quiz.

When someone asks you if there are aliens living in your town, you

A) shout "Oh, yeah!" and whip out the journal of aliens you've been keeping.

B) throw shade and ask: "Whatchu talkin' about, human?"

C) place your hands in your front pockets, act casual, and say, "Why are you asking me? It's not like I babysit them or anything. Nope, definitely never done that. Nothing to see here."

When supervising alien tykes, immediately call 911 if

A) a Stylus youngster fractures their snout.

B) a telepath fries their brain.

C) Never. Trick question.

The Klamalian you're sitting for says that her bedtime is relative because Klamalan-4 exists on a different space-time continuum than Earth. You

A) let the kid stay up all night. Sounds like perfectly good space logic to you.

B) dig the kid's logic so much that you ask her parents for twice as much money, since your hourly rate also exists on a different space-time continuum.

C) give her a fifteen-minute warning, explaining that's fifteen Earth minutes, which constitutes a finite amount of time on this planet.

The Insomarunian you're watching says she's tired and going to bed early. You

A) compliment her on being such a model child.

B) celebrate! The sooner the kid goes to bed, the sooner you can start practicing how to take the perfect selfie.

C) catch her trying to sneak out her window. Everyone knows Insomarunians never sleep. . . . Did she really think she could fool you?

Can't play a player.

The alien children you're watching have finally fallen asleep. You

A) attempt to beam yourself up with their mobile transport console.

B) see if the parents keep any lasers in their office.

C) do your homework, check in on the kids, and wait for the parents to come home.

Any chance I can pick A and B? I mean, life's short. Why limit yourself? Am I right, people?

SCORING:

If you chose mostly As: You show true potential but have not yet conquered the orientation materials. Please review them thoroughly.

If you chose mostly Bs: You show real potential. You clearly take joy in everything you do. Now just take joy in studying the orientation materials.

If you chose mostly Cs: You are ready to babysit aliens. You understand the importance of upholding intergalactic rules, demonstrate advanced maturity, and will surely study the orientation materials with diligence.

ADVICE FOR THE AGES

As an Earthling, you no doubt have heard of the terrible twos. The temper tantrums, the crying fits, the endless whining. But have you heard of the walloping ones? The ferromagnetic fours? Or the ectozoan eights? We thought not. When babysitting for aliens of all species, one must be prepared to aid children in a wide variety of formative stages. Good luck, Earthling . . . good luck.

NEWBORN (0-3 months)

You will be required to coddle, swaddle, burp, and feed these bouncing bundles of galactic joy. As with human newborns, many alien newborns are tiny helpless creatures who can barely support their own two heads. This, of course, is not the case with all alien newborns. Va'Taxian Vibra Birds, for example, age at an accelerated rate and will be full-grown within twenty-four hours of hatching.

Most alien newborns do not yet talk, so the decoding of their cries will be required. Start by doing a quick spot check for any clear comfort problems, like an antenna that's pinched in a toy hinge or a tail that's caught in a crib. In the absence of any clear and present evidence of injury, a newborn's wailing is often a sign that they are hungry, thirsty, tired, cold, hot, ill, or in need of a changed diaper. If you are unsure of how to interpret the newborn's fuss, feel free to ask the Orb. Orbs can translate more than eight thousand languages, including Infant. But an Orb will not help if you do not ask. And even then, it'll often choose to disoblige. Orbs do tend to have poor attitudes. This is why we cannot leave babysitting in the hands of the Orbs. Also, Orbs don't technically have hands.

SWADDLING A ZAGELLIAN

Swaddling a newborn ensures that the baby feels safe and warm now that they have left the pod. While swaddling can be soothing and calming for the child, swaddling a newborn alien can be challenging for sitters. Especially when that newborn is in possession of flailing tentacles. With the help of this step-by-step guide, you will become a champion Zagellian swaddle artist in no time.

STEP ONE
Lay the baby Zagellian down on their back on top of a six-pointed blanket.

STEP TWO
Place the baby's top right tentacle alongside their torso. Take the same-side pointed blanket corner (corner one), pull it securely across the Zagellian's body, and tuck it in behind the child, leaving the five remaining tentacles free to thrash around.

STEP THREE

Place the baby's top left tentacle alongside their torso. Take pointed blanket corner two, pull it securely across the Zagellian's body, and tuck it in behind the child, leaving the four remaining tentacles free to thrash around. At this point, there's a strong chance the baby's top right tentacle has broken free. If so, repeat step two, then proceed.

STEP FOUR

Place the baby's middle right tentacle alongside their torso. Take pointed blanket corner three, pull it securely across the Zagellian's body, and tuck it in behind the child, leaving the three remaining tentacles free to thrash around.

STEP FIVE

Place the baby's middle left tentacle alongside their torso. Take pointed blanket corner four, pull it securely across the Zagellian's body, and tuck it in behind the child, leaving the two remaining tentacles free to thrash around.

STEP SIX

Place the baby's lowest right and left tentacles over their tummy. Take the lowest blanket points (corners five and six), pull them up over the tentacles and tummy, and tuck them in near the chest. At this point, there's a strong chance the baby has wriggled completely out of the swaddle and has begun to flail all six tentacles about. If so, repeat steps one through six, then proceed.

STEP SEVEN

You tried to repeat steps one through six, but the Zagellian started to wail and projectile spit up blue goo. At this point, we suggest you give up the idea of swaddling. Grab six rattles, place one in each of the newborn's tentacles, and let them do their thing.

Oh, c'mon. How hard can this be? You're just making an alien burrito. Speaking of, I've got one in the microwave right now. A burrito, not an alien.

INFANTS (3-6 months)

During this next infant stage, alien babies become more socially engaged. They develop skills like giggling, cooing, and following your voice. When babysitting for an infant in this age group, we recommend reading aloud, singing lullabies, and playing with colorful plushies, toys, and, of course, astro-speed configurators. You will also be expected to feed the baby a bottle.

I got this one. my feeding game is on point.

HOW TO FEED A BABY GWARGWAR

The product of a war-torn planet, Gwargwar warriors are wary of outsiders from birth. Their untrusting nature can result in extreme feeding-time difficulties. We suggest you adhere to the following safety precautions for your own good.

1. ***Wash your hands.*** A Gwargwar infant will suspect you of carrying harmful human germs in hopes of transmitting an illness that will then weaken their immunity and wipe out their entire species. Disinfect your hands in clear sight of the infant.

2. ***Heat the bottle.*** A Gwargwar infant will assume that you're trying to burn them with an overheated bottle. To soothe their fears, heat a pot of water to a simmer, then place the bottle in the pot. Once heated, test the temperature level in front of the infant by squirting a bit of milk onto the inside of your wrist.

3. *Taste the milk.* A Gwargwar infant is fearful of being poisoned by an enemy, or even a friend. To assuage this heightened concern, you must take the first sip. Squirt a few drops of the purple milk directly from the bottle into your mouth. Be forewarned, the Gwargwar milk will taste incredibly spicy to the human tongue.

I've tasted all five levels of salsa at Luchachos and I'm still standing. Bring it on.

4. *Holding the baby.* You will find that Gwargwar babies are suspicious of any sudden moves. Approach the baby slowly with your arms in the air to show you mean no harm. To give the Gwargwar infant an added sense of security, allow them to grasp their teething spear in one hand and mini war hammer in the other. Then gently raise the child into your lap with their head resting by your elbow.

5. Burping the baby. Gwargwars react negatively to even the slightest hint of physical aggression. So post-feed burping is not welcome. If you attempt to hold the infant over your shoulder and gently pat their back, they will engage in hostile retaliation. Perhaps it's best to just set the baby Gwargwar down on their play mat and slowly back away. Most likely, the child will eventually self-release a Gwargwar burp. Heads up, Gwargwar burps are indistinguishable from Gwargwar stentorian war cries.

Well, that's sufficiently intimidating.

A note about alien pacifiers:

For some infant aliens, pacifier sucking is key to contentment between feeding times. If so, please remember to follow the alien pacifier allotment scale. Aliens with three mouths get three pacifiers, aliens with four mouths get four pacifiers, and so on and so forth. And of course, please do know which one is the alien's mouth hole.

Not as easy as one would think . . .

INFANTS (6-12 months)

During this stage of development, alien children start to sit up, roll a ball, and enjoy tactile activities, like reading *Pat the Blurble*. They also start teething, which can result in drooling, rooting, crankiness, and intense biting. Don't say we didn't warn you.

GUIDE TO BABYSITTING A TEETHING GOR-MONITE

Babysitting for a teething Gor-Monite? Good luck. While human babies in this age group start to cut a front tooth or two, baby Gor-Monites cut two hundred eleven sharp ones.

That's a whole lot of baby teeth. Does the tooth fairy get in on all that action?

Dealing with drool:

Teething human babies experience slightly increased levels of saliva production, so it's suggested that a sitter keep a bib or burp cloth handy. Gor-Monite teethers, however, produce vastly increased amounts of saliva. One might estimate several buckets' worth per hour. *Here's the deal. The whole saliva thing is gross, but kinda cool. It's basically a drool river. No, wait . . . a drool waterfall. No, I've got it . . . a saliva tsunami.*

When watching a teething Gor-Monite, you may need to place the drooling infant on top of a water-resistant tarp or in an empty water receptacle such as a birdbath, fountain, or Olympic-sized lap pool. That should help contain the excessive saliva overflow so it doesn't flood the neighbors' yard.

DIAPER DUTY

Diaper duty is indeed a reality of babysitting. It stinks. (Ha! I believe I have perfected the human culture of joke telling, have I not?) Never changed an alien's diaper before? Well, you are in for a whole lot of fun. Or is it fear? I always mix up those two Earthling terms. Oh, well.

1. Smell something? Please do something. Take a peek in the alien child's diaper. Sometimes it's a false alarm. Like the planet Jupiter, alien babies are known to be gaseous. (Yet again, I have nailed Earthling humor. Kudos to me. Kudos, I say.)

> Not really nailing the whole humor thing. But cool if we unpack that another time?

2. Don't rely simply on a foul smell. Horphons' dirty diapers smell like hot buttered popcorn at a Saturday matinee. Do not be fooled. This diaper still needs to be changed. Immediately.

3. Prepare the supplies. What you'll need:

- Alien-strength wipes

- A clean changing surface

- A garbage pail, bag, or commercial-sized dumpster to dispose of the used diaper

- A clean change of baby clothes in case of the dreaded alien blowout

- Gloves and a hazmat suit—optional but recommended when dealing with a level seven or above poop

Someone could have warned me that the poop scale actually goes to level eleven. Or as I like to call it, the Big Bang.

4. Select the properly sized clean diaper with the correct amount of appendage holes. Alien diapers come with two, three, four, or more holes for appendages.

One time, I ran out of changing supplies while watching a Titanicite. But did I panic? No. I used Wesley's old tent as a diaper. And instead of wipes? I used Olivia's favorite beach towel. See why I don't need to read all the orientation materials? It's called improvisation. And I basically rule at it.

5. Lay the baby on their back. Never leave the child unattended, as they could roll over and fall off the changing table, injuring themselves or—worse—spilling the diaper contents onto your shoes.

6. Remove any clothes covering the baby's diaper.

7. Remove the dirty diaper. To do so, simply unhinge the clasps or sticky tabs on either side. Then gently hold the baby's ankles, legs, or tentacles with one hand, and carefully slide off the dirty diaper with the other.

8. While holding up the child's legs, wipe their bottom clean. Toss the used diaper and wipes in the waste receptacle of your choice.

You should 100 percent choose a Gwargwar launch cannon. You will not regret it. Just be sure you have good aim.

8.5 This is an excellent time to note that aliens from the Yupirian Belt wear their diapers on their heads. In which case, hold up their antennae with one hand and wipe their ears clean.

8.75 This is also an excellent time to note that baby Zagellians will thrash you with their tentacles while you try to wipe their bums.

9. Grab a clean diaper and open it. Then, while holding up the child's appendages with one of your human hands, slide the diaper underneath the child using the other human hand.

10. Place the baby's appendages back down over the elastic leg edging. Use the sticky tabs, metal hinges, or galactic pressure pins provided to securely latch the diaper closed. And we mean securely.

Remember to check how the original diaper is latched before taking it off the alien. Securing a diaper can get slightly complicated when the species has five legs. When in doubt, remember that the blue tab latches to the $ sign, the green tab latches to the * sign, the red tab latches to the @ sign, the purple tab latches to the # sign—but only after you've crossed it over the + sign—and the yellow tab latches to the ! sign, but from the opposite angle. Got it? Good.

11. Reclothe the baby and wash your hands.

SPECIAL NOTE: WHAT TO DO ABOUT ALIEN DIAPER RASH

Is your alien child's bottom covered in red spots, or does it have a scaly texture? Then you might be babysitting a Utivoian. Their bottoms are naturally rough, scaly, and splotchy.

If not, then the child you are watching is most likely suffering from a case of diaper rash. Don't panic. Simply take the tube of medicated orange goo provided by the parents, squeeze it onto an Earthling kitchen spatula, and apply to the irritated area.

If you don't have a spatula, makeup brushes will work in a pinch. Although I probably wouldn't use them for your blush after.

TODDLERS (1-2 years)

You won't be sitting still while sitting for an alien toddler. Toddlers take great joy and delight in exploring their newfound walking and flying skills. And once they figure out how to run, they will keep you on your toes.

Taking a first step is a major milestone in any toddler's life. But it's an especially big deal when taken in a body that's not quite their own. Take gremlins, for example. The gremlin receives their first android body on their second birthday. Concealed behind a human toddler exterior, the gremlin can finally exit its Earthling home and explore the outside world. Its favorite new activity may quickly become trips to the local playground, where it can slide, swing, and climb its way to happiness in its new human digs. Sure, steering an android body from a midsection control deck takes some getting used to, but that's all the better for blending into Earthling society. Alien android toddlers tend to be unsteady on their humanoid feet, just like human toddlers. No one will suspect they're an alien android, as wobbling, bobbling, and tumbling while walking is quite typical for Earthlings in this age category, as well.

Way to go, little buddy!
One small step for Fritz,
one larger-sized step for gremlin-kind.

Good news: android bodies are built with an indestructible extraterrestrial alloy exterior. So while toddlers may stumble like their human counterparts, they cannot suffer from the human medical conditions known as scraped knees and skinned elbows. The little gremlin inside, however, may get tossed around within the control chamber and require a little post-outing TLC.

So you're saying I might have to kiss a fuzzy alien boo-boo? Uh, let me think about that one!

The Walloping Ones:

While human toddlers are learning to control their arms and legs, Zagellian toddlers are exploring the use of their giant tentacles. Starting around one year of age, Zagellians will thump, whack, and bash everything in sight. These tentacle tantrums are known throughout the universe as the walloping ones. If you happen to be sitting for a Zag who's going through the walloping ones, move anything valuable out of tentacle reach. This includes yourself. Once you've been sideswiped by a mischievous toddler's tentacle, you'll never be the same again.

Eh, I'm not worried. Zagellians love me. I mean, what's not to love?

PRESCHOOLERS (3-4 years)

An alien's preschool years are all about imagination, imitation, and sprouting a tail. Make-believe games, dress-up sessions, and pillow forts are all the rage. Alien children of this age also indulge in the nonstop asking of "Why?" and "What's this?" The one exception to this ceaseless line of questioning is if you're sitting for a telepath. By age three, telepaths can not only sense what you're thinking but fully comprehend it. They don't need to ask why—they can just read your mind.

For Earthlings, preschool refers to the time before one starts elementary school. On Vitreous Prime, it refers to the time before a child joins their school. Like fish, Vitreous Primeans often move through life in a coordinated group. So their preschool years can be very stressful. What if they don't live in a strong school district? What if they don't get into a good school? If you babysit for a young VP on Earth, they are most likely homeschooled. This lack of school membership may cause them to feel lonely, socially awkward, or a little skittish. Just let them know that you're happy to be there with them. This usually puts them at ease.

As long as gill boy Stewart
is rolling with me and Wes,
he's gonna be fine.

The Ferromagnetic Fours:

The science behind Blorg magnetics is too advanced for your inferior human brain. But in simple terms, around the age of four, the processing power of a Blorg's implants begins to accelerate. This causes their metallic plates to expand at a faster pace than the rest of their bodies. As a result of this imbalance, four-year-old Blorgs become highly ferromagnetic and respond strongly to magnetic fields. In others words, they're a walking, talking refrigerator magnet whom you may have to physically separate from other magnetic material.

I don't know about you, but I totally want to see this sweet, sweet magnet power in action.

ADVICE FROM LOCAL BABYSITTERS ON ALIENS' NATIVE PLANETS

"Gwargwar children will put up a fight at bedtime. Like a literal fight involving broadswords, throwing stars, and halberds. So B.Y.O.S. (bring your own shield)."

—Gbrahg, age 12, Gwar Gwar

Kali and I have reached an understanding. No scimitars after lights out. War hammers are another story. . . .

"Quiritixian kids love to lick everything in sight. It's our way of expressing joy. But on Earth, our acidic saliva will disintegrate any object it comes into contact with. So you may want to keep the kids away from any one-of-a-kind antiques and precious valuables. But feel free to have them lick away any evidence of the night's wild shenanigans before their parents get home. No evidence, no problems."

I like how you think, Rusli.   —Rusli, age 14, Quiritix

"Blorg baby throwing a temper tantrum? Even the most temperamental Blorg can't resist the sick beats of a Blorg synth-pop lullaby. Crank up the tunes and say good-bye to the tears. Lemme know if you need a playlist."

—Ayup, age 15, Blorg

Gabby D. never says no to a dance party. Just ask Joey Panther. . . .

"Babysitting kids from Luvpli is a cinch. Their favorite games include potato sniffing and banana stacking."

—Bretlus, age 13, Luvpli

Totally weird, but doable.

"Larqwans love snacking on anything sparkly. Like diamonds or chandeliers."

—Qwuign, age 15, Larqwan

That's cool, that's cool. I'm not above bedazzling a taquito.

Gabby's Secrets of a Highly Successful Babysitter

Hold up. I'm gonna pump the brakes a little on this binder. All this practical advice is super valuable and all (well, at least the couple parts I've actually read), but I'm pretty much the best babysitter I know. And if you ask me, this binder of babysitting info is lacking some secret sauce. It's all "Do this. . . . Don't do that. . . . Also don't do that." Swifty, my man, I respect your rules; I'm just not always gonna follow them. When it comes to babysitting aliens, I've got mad practical wisdom. And I'm willing to share it.

HAVE FUN

See those smiling little alien faces? See those satisfied clients? What we had here tonight is called fun. It's my number one secret to slaying as a sitter. Actually, it's kind of my number one secret to life.

DON'T PANIC

Things are gonna go wrong for sure; don't blame yourself. But how you react to a crisis? That's on you. Freaking out is not really gonna help you. So put your energy into solving the problem. Eyes to the future, my friends.

THINK BOLD

Rules, more rules, blah, blah, blah. Here's the deal.

Sometimes ya gotta get a little creative with your solutions. Dad can't make Christmas? Call in a Gor-Monite sub. Mom needs some fresh news stories? Call on your alien kids to create some local chaos. No idea is too big. Just go for it.

DON'T KEEP THE PARENTS IN THE LOOP

I seriously advise against calling the parents with an update. I find that keeping the parents in the loop only causes unnecessary alarm. And if the parents call you to check in? Tell them everything is fine. Then solve the problem yourself. The parents will never be the wiser, and you get to keep babysitting for their kid. I'd call that a win.

UNLESS THE PARENTS ARE TELEPATHIC

Like Mr. . . . . um, er—let's just call him Mr. Sky's Dad. Nothing happens to his daughter he doesn't know about. He can read Sky's mind. He can read my mind. That dude can hold a meeting in the white space of my brain. So, yeah, there's no point in trying to keep him out of the loop.

INVITE A FRIEND OVER

I may top the alien sitter charts, but I'm not doing it alone. I got my main man, Wesley, doing his thing. He has saved me so many times. It's why Swifty was willing to give him the impressive-but-fake title of senior executive liaison for intergalactic affairs. This job isn't half as much fun without him. And my sister? Olivia's always got my back. Turns out that Liv discovering I babysit aliens is one of the best things that's ever happened to the Duran sisters. She's been a huge help. So that whole rule about not having friends over while the parents are out, I'd go ahead and ignore that if I were you.

ACT FIRST, THINK LATER

This one is pretty self-explanatory. Yes, you could stand around all day and deliberate the best way to approach a crisis, but when in doubt, just dropkick the door off its hinges. I find that taking action is always the best action. So tackle that claw machine, throw that Christmas turkey, smash that security keyboard with a wrench. My solutions may not be the world's most elegant, but believe me, they work. And isn't it really about getting the job done?

DON'T BE AFRAID TO GO VORTEX AND/OR NIGHT TRAIN

Okay, so I don't exactly remember what this means. But it definitely involves throwing pocket tacos and rocking trampoline socks. Epic.

SAMPLE BABYSITTING SCHEDULE

3:00—School's out for the day

3:15—Arrive for babysitting job

3:30—Parents take their leave

3:30–3:45—After-school snack

3:45–4:15—Parentally approved games

4:15–5:15—Homework

5:15–5:45—DIY craft projects

5:45–6:15—Screen time

6:15–6:45—Dinner

6:45–7:00—Chores

7:00–7:30—Free play

7:30–7:45—Bath

7:45–8:00—Reading

8:00—Bedtime

9:00—Parents arrive home

Turn the page for what a babysitting schedule should REALLY look like!

Gabby's Schedule

3:05—Meet Wesley at Luchachos

3:29—Run in the door just as the parents need to get going

3:45-5:45—Shenanigans (often involving the alien doing something they're not supposed to). Hey, it's important to encourage the kids to become independent thinkers.

5:45-7:15—Creative problem solving and crisis management. At this point the child has most likely eaten something they shouldn't have, gone somewhere they shouldn't have, or done something they weren't supposed to do. And you? Your job is to fix anything that goes wrong before the parents come home.

7:15-7:20—No time for dinner. Just feed the kid the pocket taco you happen to be carrying around.

7:20-7:30—Dessert. There's always time for dessert.

7:30-7:45—Skip bath. Have a dance party instead.

7:45-8:00—Invent and practice a secret handshake
8:00-8:10—Kid argues and refuses to go to bed

8:10-8:58—Give in and let the kid stay up and watch Blooderella Part 4 with you

8:59—Tuck the tyke into bed and remind them to fake being asleep when their 'rents check in on them. The occasional fake snore helps sell it.

9:01—Get paid and head home before the parents notice anything is amiss

GETTING READY FOR BEDTIME

Eventually, all kids—even alien kids—need to sleep. Unless they're from Insomaru. Those children never sleep. Not a wink. But everyone else needs a little shut-eye, assuming they have eyes. So what's a sitter to do with a space tyke come sleepy time?

Be sure to get special instructions from the parents. Questions you may want to ask: What time does the alien go to sleep? Do they nap, and if so, how often? Do they sleep with a stuffy or teddy bear? Repeating the same bedtime steps as the parents should comfort the child and help them settle down.

But they don't want to go to sleep:

Alien children won't always want to exercise their sleeping option. They may seem totally tuckered out, then suddenly discover boundless energy and excuses when it's time to go to bed. They're afraid of the dark. There are Earthlings hiding in their closet. No matter what: stand firm, do not stray from the set bedtime routine for any reason, and reassure them that tomorrow is another day to play.

GABBY'S INSIDER TIP: If you've tried everything and the alien refuses to go to bed, try making a pact with them. They can stay up until you hear their parents' key in the door. Then they need to jump into bed and pretend they've been asleep for hours. That way you've got a happy kid and happy parents. So maybe the kid's a little tired the next day. . . . That falls under the category of "not your problem."

They snore:

Alien snoring can come with serious complications. Some aliens let out an innocent little whistle. But other snorers can turn into a safety hazard. If a Va'Taxian Vibra Bird starts to snore, wake them up. If you can't wake them up . . . run! Their vibrating snores are so loud, they can literally bring a house down. They can bring the neighbors' house down, too.

GABBY'S INSIDER TIP: Be sure the Va'Taxian Vibra Bird is happy before they fall asleep. If they have sweet dreams, they're less likely to destroy the world with their snoring.

They have nightmares:

Even aliens have nightmares. Mostly about the same things human kids do: they forgot the lines for their school play, their homework ate their dog, they beamed up to the wrong spaceship . . . and, of course, the dreaded suspicion that there's a human under their bed.

GABBY'S INSIDER TIP: If an alien child thinks someone or something is lurking under their bed, grab a flashlight and show the alien that there are no Earthlings hiding there. You may want to show them there are no scary Earthlings hiding in the closet or the drawers, either. Let them know the only scary Earthling in their house will be you, when you get angry, if they don't go to sleep soon. That usually works.

Stay quiet:

Once you finally get the little alien to go down, you want them to stay down. So keep your noise level to a minimum.

GABBY'S INSIDER TIP: Don't invite a klutz like Wesley to hang out after lights out. Loud chaos follows him everywhere. He's likely to wake an alien by knocking over a Mercurian vase, shattering a moon glass, or tripping over his own feet. He has freakishly large feet. Also try to keep the volume down on the TV. Unless any of the Blooderella movies are on. Obviously, you need to watch those with the volume turned all the way up.

BEDTIME STORY FOR ALIENS

For many children, their nightly bedtime routine includes a story. Or two. Or three. But you cannot tell an alien just any Earthling story. Please ensure you are up to date on your extraterrestrial tales. Here's a time-honored classic to share as you're putting your young charges to sleep.

VERNNIC AND THE BEAST

There once was a beautiful little Gor-Monite girl named Vernnic. She had skin as green as limes, teeth as sharp as spears, and rolls as gelatinous as jelly. Of all the blobs in Gor-Monia, she was the blobbiest blob of them all.

She was also extremely intelligent. And excelled at athletics. And was captain of the debate club. She was one of those tediously annoying blobs who was good at everything. She really was such a pill. Something simply had to be done about it.

One day her brother, Terinald, had had enough. He stood in his bedroom and asked his mirror, "Mirror, mirror on the wall, who's about to take a fall?" But the mirror didn't answer. Because even on Gor-Monia, mirrors are merely reflective glass. They don't speak. They're not magical. So Terinald would have to devise his own plan.

The next day, Terinald and Vernnic took a walk together across Gor-Monia's cragged, rocky terrain. After some time, they reached a nearby pit. A terrifying roar arose from within it. Terinald's plan? To feed Vernnic to the Beast.

Fortunately, the joke was on Terinald. As a top-of-her-class student, Vernnic knew all there was to know about the Beast, including its dietary preferences. The Beast adhered to a strict vegetarian diet, preferably vegan when possible. Alas, therefore and so forth, Vernnic knew she was in no danger. So the girl merely laughed at her brother and returned home. She continued to be a perfect blob who was good at everything.

Terinald realized it was no use being bothered by his sister's flawless nature. It was best to just bask in the glow of perfection, as with the Hemsworth brothers.

The moral of the story? You just keep doing you, even if it means being annoyingly perfect. But let's hope it doesn't. I prefer friends with a few quirks.

ALIEN BEDTIME ROUTINE QUIZ

Getting aliens to bed isn't easy. Take this quiz to see how your zzzzzzz skillz match up.

How far ahead should you warn an alien child that bedtime is imminent?

A) Thirty minutes ahead of time

B) Five minutes ahead of time

C) Fifteen minutes ahead of time

Answer: C. Unless you're sitting for a time-traveling alien. Earthling time is totally irrelevant to those ones, as they will travel in a continuous time loop back to one hour before bedtime. I knew the answer! Boom! Question closed.

How should you help an alien child settle down for bedtime?

A) Make up a catchy song about bedtime to help the young alien focus

B) Read them a bedtime story

C) Take away their Ancient Hammer of Gwargwar

Answer: All of the above. I'm acing this quiz. Is this all you got?

If humans wear PJs with spaceships and aliens on them, what do aliens wear?

    A) PJs with humans on them

    B) PJs with stripes

    C) Footed pajamas. Or in the case of Ligtorites, three-footed pajamas.

Answer: Sorry, I zoned out. I started thinking about how alien pajamas must come in a crazy number of sizes. It's not like you can go with one-size-fits-all. You've got your pint-sized fairies; you've got your colossal blobs. Wait—do Gor-Monite blobs even wear pajama bottoms? They don't exactly have feet. Huh, the mysteries of the universe really are endless.

Do aliens sleep with a night-light on?

    A) Yes. Even aliens are afraid of the dark.

    B) Yes, but only the species who don't have phosphorescent scales

    C) Some aliens are nocturnal, so they go to sleep with a day-light on.

Answer: Sorry, still thinking about the last question. . . . What about nightcaps? Do most aliens wear those, or is that just a Swifty thing?

ALIENS LIVING ON
EARTH LESSON PLAN

GABBY,
I TRUST YOU UNDERSTAND THE IMPORTANCE OF
INSTRUCTING ALIEN YOUTH ON THE FOLLOWING DIRE
ISSUES WHILE YOU'RE BABYSITTING THEM. I'M COUNTING
ON YOU, GABBY. INITIATE IMPORTANT EARTH LESSONS
IMMEDIATELY.

FONDLY,
PRINCIPAL SWIFT

P. P. S.

1. The history of Earth

Sorry, no can do. Life's short; history's in the past.
I'm teaching these aliens how to live in the now.

2. How to speak the Queen's English

No offense, Principal, but you can't blend into Earth
talking like a duke from a PBS drama. I'm teaching these
aliens the dope art of middle school lingo.

3. Proper Earthling table manners

Nailed it . . . if by table manners you mean drinking
directly from the horchata dispenser.

4. The importance of rule following

Look at me—I live a pretty good life. And have I been going around following all the rules my whole life? No. So why would I tell the kids they have to?

5. The practice of speaking only when spoken to

Lucky for you, I take my babysitting duties very seriously. Which is why I would never teach an alien kid this. If you want to fit in on Earth, you've got to speak your mind. Take it from me.

6. How to blend in with Earthlings

Alien principal said what? Sorry, no can do. I mean, I don't want anyone getting caught or anything. But if you want to be happy on our planet, you've got to do your thing. Stay unique.

7. The art of the Earthling dance (Might I suggest starting with the waltz and the minuet?)

Now lemme ask, are you trying to ruin these kids' social lives? When it comes to dance, leave the moves to me. You're talking to the girl who made murdering a dance floor a crime. That was a joke, Swifty. Dancing is not actually a crime on Earth as it is on some planets. But if it was, I'd be guilty. Cuz I'm the sickest dancer to hit Havensburg in basically forever.

8. The importance of getting along with others

Already ahead of you on this one. When I got to Havensburg, I had nothing. But babysitting gave me purpose; it gave me friends. My alien kids and I are tight.

9. Self-defense against birds (Those vile creatures will be the end of me.)

Told ya, Swifty, that's not why I duct-taped your car. I was trying to . . . You know what, never mind. Sure, I'm happy to teach Jeremy how to duct-tape your car. Something tells me he's gonna get a kick out of pulling some sweet, sweet pranks on you.

10. The vital Earthling act of working as a team

Squad goals? You came to the right place. Sky, Stewart, Fritz, Kali, Jeremy, me, Wes, Olivia—we're like the band that makes beats come together.

Top Ten Things I Learned About Teen Culture from My Earthling ~~Babysitter~~ Friend

Forget Principal Swift's learning list. I love teen stuff. And my new Earthling BFF, Gabby Duran, is a real human teenage girl! Not only is she way better than my last best friend (a stuffed owl, who, by the way, was really mean), but Gabby has taught me so much about teen stuff. Until Gabby took me to school with her, I didn't even know how much there was to know. She's the best!

Telepathic girl say what?!

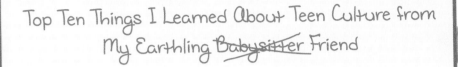

Sky

1. Earthling teen culture is everything I imagined and more.

2. The hoodie is the most versatile of all the teen fashion. A teen can never have too many. Colorful sweaters with zippers in front are also acceptable.

3. When wearing overalls, only fasten one shoulder. Fastening both is a major middle school no-no.

My work here is done.

4. Youth overnight sleeping events are the most fun ever. Especially if you pull pranks on a security guard. It's an epic teen rite of passage.

5. There are two amazing Earthlings named Drake, both worthy of teenage praise. Everyone's favorite, Sir Francis Drake, famous sea captain and explorer. And also a rapper. Who knew?

6. Emojis are the key to successful teen human communication.

7. Rocking your first school dance is all about being with your friends, arriving in stretch-limo style, and claiming total dance supremacy with some sweet moves. Check me out, slaying the Boxer. Also, dancing with a human like Wesley is superior to dancing with Riblet McSkullface.

8. Never say "Dope to the max." The word "dope" expresses the maximum level of dopeness possible.

9. Brightly colored shoes make the outfit.

10. Having friends like Gabby and Wesley makes teenage life a million times better. For the first time since I got to Earth, I feel like I really belong.

BATH-TIME BASICS

Alien parents may request that you give their offspring a bath before bedtime. This nightly routine not only removes all the caked-on goo, glob, and dirt they attracted during the day, it aids children in falling asleep. While some alien children love a good scrub-a-dub-dub, others cringe at the thought.

"Scrub-a-dub-dub"? Who says that?

Here are a few tips to aid in the accomplishment of a successful bath time:

Chilling with Yuparians

Yuparians hail from a planet covered in frozen tundra, so they prefer to bathe in water at near-freezing temperatures. For best results, fill the bathtub three quarters of the way with ice cubes, then top off with the coldest water possible from the spout.

Cleaning Your Gor-Monite Charge

A Gor-Monite bathing in human form is like an Earthling showering
in a raincoat. There's no point. Therefore, for Gor-Monites, bath
time means blob time. How does an Earthling sitter manage that?
A drive-through car wash would be an excellent solution were
it not for the high risk of disclosing our secret presence. So let's
move on to our second-best bathing option. You'll need a kiddie
pool, a full-sized mop, and a garden hose. Blow up the inflatable
pool, then fill it halfway with water so it doesn't overflow once
the Gor-Monite gets in. Once the blob has entered the pool, scrub
the child down with a mop. Be sure to get the dirt out from under
all the gelatinous folds and rolls. Then rinse off the soap with the
hose's nozzle set to high-pressure spray.

To switch it up, I sometimes let Jeremy play in the
backyard lawn sprinkler, then hose him off as he
nosedives on a Slip 'N Slide.

Self-Bathing Amphibaliens

If you're sitting for an Amphibalien, you're off the hook. Amphibaliens have a tongue that extends to many times the length of their body. This physical feature allows them to self-clean, catch flies on the quick, or do both simultaneously.

Don't know if I should be grossed out or impressed. But you just keep being you, Froggy.

Snacking and Bathing Snarlons

Due to the sensitive nature of their mothlike wings, Snarlons bathe in a solution made up of two parts tomato soup and one part bubble bath. Snarlons also enjoy eating grilled cheese in the bathtub. So always have one at the ready.

Doubling Down on Bath Time

Bath time for android-piloting aliens is a two-part process: first android, then gremlin. For the android body, apply the parent-provided soap solution to a soft sponge, then swab in a circular motion. Be sure to dry thoroughly to avoid rust formation. Next, carefully help the gremlin out of the midriff android control center and place the little guy in a three-quart soup pot filled with lukewarm water. Shampoo his fur. Scrub his head. Don't forget to wash behind his antennae. Yes, all four of them. Hold a towel over the alien while he shakes off the excess water. Finally, run a brush through his fur to prevent tangles and knots from forming.

I've noticed with Fritz, there's not a lot of ventilation happening in the ol' android control center. So it can get a little ripe in there—like a middle school locker room after basketball practice ripe. So you're gonna want to lift up the android's shirt and let that stinky steering deck air out overnight.

ALIEN BATH-TIME QUIZ

Can android bodies get wet? Can Blurbles multiply in water? Are you supposed to exfoliate Rvthicans' scales? It's time to test how well you know your alien bath-time routines!

When giving a Praxian Fairy a bath, which do you do?

A) Use a teacup or coffee mug for a bathtub

B) Add one drop of bath gel for a six-ounce teacup and two drops for a twelve-ounce mug

C) Remember to rinse behind their wings

D) Ha! You think you can catch a Praxian Fairy long enough to give them a bath? You have much to learn, Earthling.

When giving a Vitreous Primean a bath, what do you do?

A) Splash them with bubble bath

B) Scrub-a-dub-dub with a loofah

C) Play with a rubber ducky

D) None of the above. Vitreous Primeans hail from a water planet. Bathing seems a little redundant when you sleep in a water tank.

Which of the following is considered a Gwargwar bath toy?

A) A spear

B) A mace

C) A nagaika

D) Anything a Gwargwar feels like taking into the bathtub

How do you clean a baby Va'Taxian Vibra Bird?

A) Use your kitchen sink as a tub

B) Preen their feathers using your own mouth and feet, as if you were their mama bird

C) Chirp sweet nothings in their ear

D) Due to the hyper-accelerated growth rate of Va'Taxian Vibra Birds, this answer changes daily.

When bathing a two-headed Ytuvian, what do you do?

A) Shampoo and condition each head one at a time

B) Shampoo and condition both heads simultaneously

C) Alternate days. Rinse, lather, repeat for head one on even days of the month. Rinse, lather, repeat for head two on odd days of the month.

D) Make a game-time decision. Ytuvians are pretty chill.

When giving a Mungo, like Daria, a bath, what do you do?

    A) Wash in warm water

    B) Hand wash in cold water with like colors

    C) Tumble dry on low heat

    D) None of the above. Mungos are dry-clean only.

SCORING:

If you chose mostly As: You show true potential but have not yet conquered the orientation materials. Please review them thoroughly.

If you chose mostly Bs: You show real potential. You clearly take joy in everything you do. Now just take joy in studying the orientation materials.

If you chose mostly Cs: You show some potential. You have a lot of creative ideas about babysitting; you just need to read the orientation materials to better understand the needs of alien youngsters.

If you chose mostly Ds: You are ready to attempt bathing your alien charge. You understand the importance of upholding intergalactic rules, demonstrate advanced maturity, and will surely study the orientation materials with diligence.

Traits of a Baller Babysitter
by Jeremy

Swift is a silly man with uncool ideas and really long legs. I'm the one who knows what makes a babysitter baller. Check out my list of cool babysitter requirements:

1) Brings me nachos

2) Thinks studying is less important than fun

3) Lets me do anything I want

4) Takes me to the drive-through

5) Throws parties while the adults are out

6) Doesn't believe in bedtimes

6.5) MY BUTT of course, Jeremy's answer to everything

7) Teaches me how to throw down Earth slang

8) Always sides with me over the Orb

9) Thinks I'm baller

10) Is named Gabby Duran

Smell ya later,
Jeremy

Jeremy wrote that? It's confirmed. I love my super-awesome, life-fulfilling babysitting gig.

SUSIE GLOVER'S TOP FIVE ACTIVITIES WHILE BABYSITTING

Gabby here. This is a screenshot of Susie Glover's babysitting app. She may only have a 4.99-star rating for babysitting skills, but I would give her a perfect five out of five stars for boring skills. Read her activity tips, then do the opposite.

Susie Glover: Super Sitter (trademark pending)

At Susie Glover: Super Sitter (trademark pending), our motto is "Safety before fun." Typical activities I might engage your child in include . . .

Whisper origami
Children enjoy the restorative art of Japanese paper-folding methods while listening to the muted sounds of the human whisper.

Investigation: Punctuation
Children rise to the challenge of proper punctuation by investigating situations.

 Like CSI: Punctuation? I'll take a hard pass.

Hopscotching word games
Children love the invigorating challenge of vocabulary expansion combined with the physical exhilaration of hopscotch.

I prefer butterscotch to hopscotch.

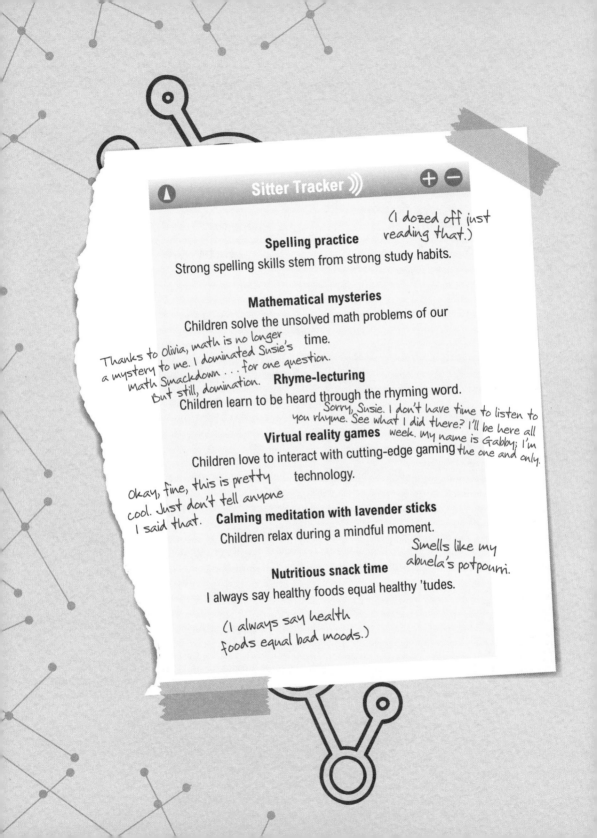

Sitter Tracker))

Spelling practice

Strong spelling skills stem from strong study habits.

(I dozed off just reading that.)

Mathematical mysteries

Children solve the unsolved math problems of our time.

Thanks to Olivia, math is no longer a mystery to me. I dominated Susie's Math Smackdown . . . for one question. But still, domination.

Rhyme-lecturing

Children learn to be heard through the rhyming word.

Sorry, Susie. I don't have time to listen to you rhyme. See what I did there? I'll be here all week. My name is Gabby; I'm the one and only.

Virtual reality games

Children love to interact with cutting-edge gaming technology.

Okay, fine, this is pretty cool. Just don't tell anyone I said that.

Calming meditation with lavender sticks

Children relax during a mindful moment.

Smells like my abuela's potpourri.

Nutritious snack time

I always say healthy foods equal healthy 'tudes.

(I always say health foods equal bad moods.)

SATISFYING AN ALIEN SNACK ATTACK

Below is an inventory of galactic gourmet foods frequently found in alien kitchens. These may be served as species-specific snacks to alien children in response to the oft-whined phrase "I'm hungry." Please note many of the extraterrestrial edibles are inedible for humans. Do not attempt to eat them. Horrible side effects may be suffered. Likewise, aliens are allergic to many Earthling foods. Do not feed anything to an alien child that does not appear on the alien-approved consumables list.

As a babysitter, you have a basic right to rummage through the pantry in search of a snack. Some parents even say things like "Feel free to help yourself to anything in the refrigerator," which is basically adult-speak for "Feel free to finish our gallon of rocky road ice cream" and "We would love if you demolished the fresh cupcakes we made for the school bake sale tomorrow." Sometimes babysitting feels like you're getting paid to eat other people's junk food. Am I right?

But take it from me: raiding the kitchen while babysitting aliens is a whole different thing. Each alien species consumes a diet specific to their planet. And let me tell you, some of that alien food is super weird. Which only makes me want to try it more.

Illumibites

This bright green gummy candy is popular with Gor-Monite youth. When the candy is consumed, the luminosity of it on your tongue fills the room.

Also, it tastes like maple syrup and lightning.

Boblolob beans

This Gor-Monite candy contains Gor-Monozine Neokine, an alien chemical a hundred times more powerful than anything the human brain can process. It makes you so happy you lose all control and feel like you're going to explode. Do not eat this candy.

You really think I'd do something that irresponsible? It's like you don't even know me at all. Of course I wouldn't eat it. I'd just feed it to my sister.

Zzyrcxicles

These frozen treats from the Yupirian Belt combine the sweet flavor of elbow blossoms with subtle notes of strawberry jelly.

Human hair

If a Gor-Monite eats hair, the alien will shape-shift into the human whose hair he plucked.

Jeremy, my man, you are what you eat.

Pritfinirols

These are the best, most delicious, most delectable desserts in all the universe. Handmade in the ovens of Praxian Fairies, they are unfortunately but the size of a piece of dust. My deepest apologies, Earthling, but you won't be able to taste them.

Blirnzels

These small salty snacks from the Jikchxl galaxy make for a favorite refreshment at athletic events. They taste like butter and picture frames and are not acceptable for human consumption.

I want you to remember that you left me with no choice but to try these.

Puffglot

A large Zagellian pastry, this tasty treat takes two hands (or one tentacle) to eat.

Gor-Monite breath mints

No ordinary breath enhancer, these delicious mints provide a cool, refreshing peppermint punch that lasts throughout the day. Also, as they are made with sodium silicate, the mints prevent the unfortunate explosion and/or melting of cells by blocking the molecular structure assimilation that occurs when a Gor-Monite consumes an object.

When babysitting a Gor-Monite, never leave home without these bad boys. You'll find them in a container cleverly labeled "Just Plain mints," because that's not suspicious.

Blorkdus

A dessert often consumed by Blorgs, these flat trapezoid cookie-like snacks taste like old books and fizzle in one's mouth as they dissolve. They are delicious.

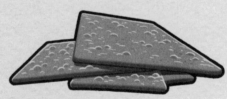

Kelp

On their native Vitreous Prime, Vitreous Primeans consume kelp straight from the sea. Those living in Havensburg grow fresh kelp in their window box planters and cultivate it in their gardens. Kelp tastes like kale or spinach and is safe for humans to eat.

It might be safe, but it's not good. I prefer to bring fish boy Stewart roasted seaweed snack packs from the store. They're kind of like the tortilla chips of the sea.

Nutrient slurry

Originally developed for mid-combat consumption, this Gwargwar snack food provides a full day's serving of vitamins, proteins, and nutrients in the convenience of a shake. By law, every Gwargwar is required to devour at least one slurry per day to maintain their body's battle-readiness. The slurry contains dietary enrichments not found on Earth. So while nourishing for Gwargwars, the slurry is toxic to humans and will result in blue skin, hand hair, and cry-snorting.

Thanks and all, but I think I'm gonna stick with horchata.

Liquefied beetle

Zagellian baby food may resemble the sticky blueberry syrup Earthlings use at the meal of breakfast, but do not pour it on your Earthling pancakes. It's actually liquefied Zagellian beetle parts and should only be consumed by creatures with six or more tentacles. Warning: Consumption of this blue goo by a human could cause spontaneous tentacle growth.

Okay, that is way grosser than I expected.

Moon cheese and crackers

Self-explanatory

Va'Taxian wiggle worms

To feed a baby Va'Taxian Vibra Bird, simply chew some Va'Taxian wiggle worms in your mouth, swallow, then then regurgitate the partly digested slug worms into the nestling's mouth. Don't be grossed out: chewing and regurgitating Earth gummy worms is also acceptable in a pinch.

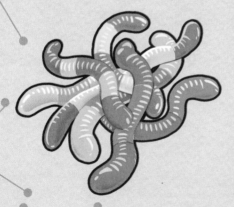

Yeah, sorry, still gross.

Gor-Monite cleanse

This black tar-like sludge rids Gor-Monites of sluggish feelings, making them feel more youthful and vibrant. Caution: The cleanse also purges a Gor-Monite's shape-shifting memory deposit. Do back up your shape-shifting source materials pre-cleanse. Otherwise, you will be unable to shift back into any previously taken shape.

Yo, Swifty! If you want to blend in seamlessly with Earth culture, you're gonna have to lay off the weird space food. It's time you indulged in a real Earthling delicacy. I present to you the Funky Food Fiesta. Known as the greatest meal in the galaxy, the Triple-F is the single best combination of food to appear in one dish. Ever. And I've had the Luchachos combo platter, so that's saying a lot. Here's the recipe:

1 jar/container each:
- pickles
- jelly
- peanut butter
- whipped cream
- hot pepper mix

1 box Sugar-Frosted Blammo Bombs

1 habanero pepper

2 bananas

1 English muffin

3/4 lb chorizo

Blend in ketchup, mustard, and chocolate syrup

Top with sprinkles. Enjoy!

THE BUSINESS OF BABYSITTING ALIENS

GETTING YOUR ALIEN BABYSITTING BUSINESS STARTED

The time has come to discuss the business side of babysitting: the finances, the scheduling, the obtaining of customers, and so forth. There are numerous ways for a junior high school person to find typical human babysitting clients:

- Hang up flyers in coffee shops, grocery stores, and clothing boutiques around town.

- Advertise on your quaint little World Wide Web.

- Pass out business cards.

- Register with a certified babysitting service.

- Network with friends and family who have children, and ask your parents to inform their friends, as well.

- Search on job sites for available nanny posts and babysitter listings.

To point out the obvious—because the human brain does not always grasp it on its own (not your fault; you're merely an inferior species)—you cannot use any of the above client recruitment methods for aliens without jeopardizing the secret of alien existence on Earth. You can only obtain extraterrestrial clients through the means that follow:

- Principal Swift awarding you an assignment

- Alien-to-alien word of mouth**

- And . . . that's all.

Sounds great . . . except if Swifty tries to bail on Earth, ghosts all your calls, then hides in a garbage heap. Kinda problematic, since he's the guy who makes it all happen. The alien babysitting system breaks down without him. None of my clients call me back, no replacement Swift shows up, and I don't get to babysit, which is basically the one thing that's giving my life meaning. So, yeah, Swifty, you're not allowed to leave again. Like ever. You're irreplaceable, big guy.

**Telepathic aliens can also obtain your name and identification by reading the minds of your other clients.

HOW TO BILL YOUR ALIEN CLIENTS

Before you accept a babysitting job, discuss the monetary arrangements with the alien parents. Establish your hourly compensation rate up front, and mention any special circumstances that might incur an extra cost. For example:

Additional children

It's reasonable to charge more for an additional child. Extra kids equal extra work, which equals extra pay. Now you may be asking yourself, what about an extra head? If an alien child has two heads, does this count as one child or two? And what if the alien child has four legs? Or six arms?

According to the Intergalactic Babysitting Code of Practices (IBCP), if an alien child is two-headed, the sitter should charge for one and a half children. If the alien child has four legs, the sitter should charge for one and a quarter children. If the alien child has three heads and eight legs, run!

No way. There's no turning back in babysitting. Warrior Kali taught me to face my fears head-on. Or, in this case, three heads-

Pet pay

If you're asked to watch a pet instead of a child, charge your normal base rate. Intergalactic pets can be as much trouble as intergalactic children, if not more. If you're asked to watch a pet in addition to a child, then feel free to ask for auxiliary pet pay. Kids plus pets equal double trouble.

I don't know what's worse: getting pooped on by an alien bird or swallowing an invisible lizard egg. Either way, trust me on this: pet peril pay is the real deal.

Surge pricing

Surge pricing for popular times and holidays when demand is high is considered an acceptable practice. Such celebrations include Praxian Opposite Day, Blorgian Excellence in Being the Best Festival, and the Gwargwar Celebration of Telling It Like It Is.

Hazard pay

At times, babysitting for aliens comes with a degree of physical risk. But what's a little pain and suffering when it means you get to be an intergalactic babysitter? As they say on Gwar Gwar, comfort is for weaklings.

However, there may be cases of the most extreme jeopardy that require you to purchase protective gear. Since Quiritixian aliens spit up acidic saliva that disintegrates everything on contact, you may charge extra to buy gloves, a mask, and a hazmat suit. Likewise, children allowed to play with warrior-grade weapons often inflict accidental bodily harm. Feel free to charge more for the purchase of armor, or request reimbursement for medical bills that may arise from being pierced by a spear.

Unfortunately, getting caught in the middle of a game of Blorgian Extreme Punchy Arm does not count as true bodily injury, so you cannot charge extra for it. You can only punch back. Hard.

If I ever have to sit for humans again, maybe I'll charge a boredom fee, since it's so much less hazardous and less interesting than sitting for aliens.

Tutoring

It is expected that you will encourage alien children to complete all their homework before proceeding with a fun time of Earthling TV watching or playing outside. This is a responsibility that is included in your hourly rate. However, insomuch as a parent may request that you go above and beyond and tutor their child in a specific academic subject at which you excel, you may ask for supplemental tutorial pay.

Homework and I have an "I don't like you, you don't like me" relationship. So it's gonna be a big nope on tutoring. Who do you think I am, Susie Glover?

Currency

Remember to ask to be paid in Earthling dollar units (also known to Earthlings as the Benjamins, the moolah, the cheddar, or the cold hard cash). Many alien parents are used to paying in the currency native to their home planet.

Moon rocks and xlactics may buy you a three-course meal on an asteroid, but they won't get you far at Luchachos.
Plus, twenty dollars' worth of moon rocks really weighs down your backpack.

SUIT UP

Many Earthling professions require the wearing of a uniform. Take, for example, the human sport of baseball. The human in charge of hitting balls wears a jersey, the human who works as a hot dog liaison wears an apron, and the human who works as the furry captain of crowd entertainment wears what is referred to as a mascot costume. All those humans dress for success. Likewise, one who works as a sitter to aliens should take care to wear the appropriate gear. Your clothing should allow you to be active and comfortable while it provides protection from intergalactic elements. Here are a few suggestions for appropriate attire:

- Protective eyewear in case of projectile goo

- A shirt you don't mind getting covered in spills, dirt, and glitter dust

- Dungarees that can withstand acidic spit-up and Gwargwar war paint

- Sensible shoes for chasing after Praxian Fairies

- Hair in a librarian bun to prevent little tentacles from pulling on it

- Muted colors so as not to excite the children

GABBY'S SIGNATURE SITTER STYLE

You're not gonna catch me rolling out in that. You can't feel good if you don't look good. Besides, someone needs to teach these alien kids about Earth fashion, and I can tell you right now it's not going to be Swifty. That guy mastered the art of wearing a dress shirt under an argyle cardigan under a sport coat, topped off with a bow tie. Who dresses like that? Aliens, that's who.

Mix and match! Patterns, bold colors, bright plaids, checkerboard, leopard print, camouflage, and glittering gold suits are all acceptable—and awesome! Here are a few of my other favs:

- Hoodie—Never leave home without one.
- Wide-leg pants or shorts—They say "comfy but cute" with attitude.
- Funky belt—For an added touch of flair.
- Bucket hat—Brings home my whole hip-girl-you-can't-help-loving vibe.
- Sweet kicks—I've got a soft spot for bright sneaks and high-tops.
- Loose long hair
- Bold nail polish—Kids gotta learn about colors somehow, right?
- Floral backpack

INTERGALACTIC TROUBLESHOOTING

EMERGENCY INSTRUCTIONS

In case of an alien child emergency, DO NOT:

- Call 911
- Call the police
- Call the fire department
- Call an Earthling doctor
- Call a neighbor
- Call your mom

DO:

- Call Principal Principal Swift
- Call the alien's parents

- Call Wesley
  - Kick down the door

more confident? Never really been an issue for me. I know I pretty much rock at everything. Besides, how hard can it be to throw a bandage on an alien boo-boo? Or tell a kid with six legs to "walk it off"? I've got this. . . .

FIRST AID FOR ALIENS

Do you have your cosmic CPR certification? Are you an expert at extraterrestrial first aid? Do you know alien poison control protocol? If not, be sure to complete your multiplanetary emergency training before proceeding with your babysitting duties. If you have the proper skills, not only will alien parents feel more confident trusting you with their children, but you'll feel more confident when it comes to watching wee ones.

Certified intergalactic alien first aid classes can be taken through Principal Principal Swift, a Gor-Monite Orb, or the Intergalactic Red Cross. Classes even include a nifty completion certificate and cover the following topics:

- How to bandage a sprained antenna
- How to clean a scraped scale
- So your alien got a papercut
- Do Praxian Fairies bruise easily?
- Can a Vitreous Primean get sunburned?
- Does a Larqwan vomit green?
- So your Blorg has boils
- Do alien bones break?
- What to do when a Zagellian pulls a tentacle. Hint: Rest. Ice. Compression. Evacuation. (RICE)
- How to give the Heimlich to a Va'Taxian Vibra Bird

A QUICK GUIDE TO DIAGNOSING ALIEN ILLNESSES

While the Orb is programmed with medical procedures for a variety of life-forms, its unreliable attitude means you might be on your own. Use the chart below to help diagnose your ill alien child:

If the ill alien is a Gor-Monite, continue to **2A**.

If the ill alien is a telepath, continue to **2B**.

If the ill alien is a Zaroodan Invisi-lizard, continue to **2C**.

2A

If the symptoms include wayward facial hair, go to **3A**.

If the symptoms include sneezing, go to **3B**.

If the symptoms include pain-shrieking, go to **3C**.

If the symptoms include a headache, go to **3D**.

2B

If the symptoms include the rambling of disparate facts, go to **4A**.

2C

If the symptoms include lying around all day, go to **5A**.

3A

Diagnosis: Your Gor-Monite is growing a stress-stache. Any kind of excessive stress may cause the hair follicles on a Gor-Monite's face to go crazy. A stressed-out Gor-Monite will literally break out in a mustache, no matter their age.

Symptoms: Spontaneous upper-lip hair growth

Treatment: Do not attempt to shave off a stress-stache. It will grow back thicker. The only treatment is to permanently remove the source of the tension. We assume that, as the babysitter, you will play no role in the introduction of such unnecessary stress—only in its elimination.

Sheesh, you ask a kid to keep one little secret and look what happens.

3B

Diagnosis: Your Gor-Monite has the flu.

Symptoms: Sneezing, tooth loss, ashen skin, dark under-eye circles, lethargy, and a sense that everything is too scratchy

Treatment: An infusion of healthy Gor-Monite cells will energize the immune system. This painful process requires both the donor and the recipient to undergo a medical procedure involving a very, very long needle.

Note: If a human were to ingest Gor-Monite mucus, it would flood their neurons, thereby changing their chemical makeup, accelerating synaptic activity and making their brain more efficient.

All I know is that a Gor-Monite's snot is wet, purple, and totally dope. I accidentally swallowed Jeremy's nose jelly and next thing I know, I'm a super genius. Gotta say, felt pretty good. Olivia must feel like that all the time. I'm weirdly looking forward to Jeremy getting sick again.

3C

Diagnosis: Your Gor-Monite has the Darkness. When something dramatic happens to a Gor-Monite, they enter the Darkness. Overcome with grief, they turn into a shell of themselves.

Symptoms: Whimpering, trash dwelling, pain-shrieking, and ear farts. The final stage of the Darkness is full-body gooping. *I know it's not nice to mock other people's pain, but you've gotta see an ear fart. It's hilarious.*

Treatment: There is no known general treatment. Every Gor-Monite is different. Some never recover; they remain a goopy pile of gelatinous blob forever.

I don't know where you're at with the whole "no treatment" thing, but—non-humblebrag—I singlehandedly rescued Swifty from the Darkness. I told him he was irreplaceable to me. And I meant it. Babysitting aliens gave me purpose. Or more like Principal Swift did. So un-Darknessing him was the least I could do.

3D

Diagnosis: Your Gor-Monite has brain freeze.

Symptoms: Sudden-onset headache

Treatment: Your Gor-Monite has consumed the Earthling treat of froyo too quickly. Request that they eat dessert at a slower pace.

4A

Diagnosis: Your telepath fried their brain.

Symptoms: Side-to-side head jerking, muttering a nonstop stream of disparate facts

Treatment: The touch telepath is suffering from a systematic overload of their synaptic pathways. You must create a pressure-release matrix so the overabundance of thoughts has a place to go. If the thoughts are human, the thought transfer process must be to a human brain. If the thoughts are Praxian Fairy, the thought transfer process must be to a Praxian Fairy. And so on and so forth. . . .

Okay, in my defense, I didn't mean to give Sky brain fry. Who knew middle schoolers had so much angst?

5A

Diagnosis: Your Zaroodan Invisi-lizard is pregnant.

Symptoms: General malaise, lying around, low energy, seems off all day

Treatment: None! Just wait for the eggs to hatch. Invisi-lizards lay their eggs in a warm, saucy environment and simultaneously shed their skin. And then congratulations are in order. A baby Invisi-lizard makes a lovely addition to any family.

Thanks to this lizard, I'm never eating carnitas again. Oh, who am I kidding? I'm having carnitas for lunch.

SEVENTY-EIGHT RULES FOR BABYSITTING ALIENS

Rule 1

Discretion is imperative. Never tell anyone that you
babysit aliens. The first rule of alien babysitting is never
talk about alien babysitting. *Busted. But hear me
out: babysitting aliens is way
better when you have someone
to talk to about everything.*

Rule 2

Do not ignore rule number one. Under any circumstances.
Revealing our secret will result in the immediate mind wipe
of you and those you've told. Also, you'll be fired and never
get to babysit aliens again. So there.

Rule 3

Inform Principal Swift without delay if anything goes wrong.

Rule 4

Do not leave alien children unattended.
You are being paid to watch them. And we are
watching you. (Insert evil alien laugh here.)

Rule 5

Never raid an alien's fridge for snacks.
Trust us, you don't want to eat what's in there.

Rule 6

Never take a flying saucer for a joyride—
even if the keys are left on the counter.

Rule 7

It is strictly prohibited to bring an alien to school with you.

Rule 8

No, not even for show-and-tell.

Rule 9

No, not even for the talent show.

Rule 10

As a babysitter, you are a guest in an alien family's home. Never rummage around, search through, or scrabble about the domicile while the parents are out. Unless given specific permission, do not open any closed doors, scour any hidden passageways, or ferret around any alien attics. There's no unseeing what you might see. And you could see a lot of things—some of it really quite interesting and mind-blowing. You'd probably find it fascinating. Even glorious. You're still not allowed to snoop.

Rule 11

Never challenge someone from Yoglatch to a thumb war.

Rule 12

Trolusious wrestling is only funny if someone loses an eyeball.

Rule 13
If a Ligtorite asks to eat a piece of rye bread,
only feed them the crusts.

Rule 14
Never release an alien pet from its cage.
Without a doubt, disaster will ensue. Every. Single. Time.

Rule 15
Wear protective clothing and masks
while interacting with a Larqwan.

Rule 16
Do not allow a Utivoian to play with a hula hoop.
Trust us, the results are not pretty.

Rule 17
No vlogs, journals, or diary entries about babysitting aliens.

Rule 18
Always burp a Forician baby outside the domicile.
Their burp winds are of a stronger force than an Earth
tornado. We warned you.

Rule 19
Humans are gross. *Not really a rule. Did Jeremy write this one?*

Rule 20

Don't leave an alien child alone too long, especially a
Gor-Monite. They will grow deeply paranoid and shape-shift
into a random household object. And good luck finding
them then.

Rule 21

The mischievous imps from the third planet in the Kitor star
group are master mind manipulators. When sitting for one,
do not trust the reality you see.

Rule 22

Add two tablespoons of red chemical powder to every
seventeen ounces of liquid in the water tank of an alien
who hails from Vitreous Prime.

Rule 23

Natives of Vitreous Prime require access to breathable water
at all times. If a Vitreous Primean chooses to exit their
water chamber, the wearing of a portable breathing collar
is required. Each handy collar contains exactly one thirty-
minute allotment of breathable water.

Rule 24

Aliens from Horphon hate the color peach.
It is forbidden to wear this hideous shade in their presence.

Rule 25

Do not share information with a telepath child that you don't desire their parents to learn. Do not involve a telepath child in any Earthling shenanigans you don't want their parents to become aware of. They will find out. And they won't be happy.

Rule 26

Look both ways before crossing the street on the back of a Vpituian T'yaxian.

Rule 27

Do not play freeze tag with one who hails from Luvpli.

Rule 28

Never take a Yirkin child to a hardware store.

Okay, well, now I'm just tempted. . . .

Rule 29

Don't spend the emergency money on anything except emergencies.

Rule 30

Tacos are never an emergency.

Rule 31

When sitting for a Yullilian, the thermostat must remain at 59 degrees Fahrenheit.

Rule 32

Do not throw a Gor-Monite a bud day party.

Rule 33

Never let a three-eyed Zipulian leave the house
without sunglasses.

Rule 34

Never ask an alien child to take you on a visit
to their native planet. Unsanctioned intergalactic
babysitting travel is strictly forbidden.

Rule 35

Do not invite friends over while babysitting.
Also do not invite enemies over.

Rule 36

To counteract a Chiplupean sneeze attack,
administer two tablespoons of vanilla extract
and take the child for a prolonged bike ride.

Rule 37

Kids from Csivteon-7 do not express emotions,
yet they do experience them. Ask logic-based questions
to uncover the nature of what they're feeling.

Rule 38

Children from the Balitorian Belt shouldn't watch soccer.
I won't go into details here. I'll just say, "You're welcome."

Rule 39

When clipping a Titanicite's toenails, distract them with
country music. Something about the Earthling tales of broken
hearts and broken-down trucks soothes them.

Rule 40

Never party with the aliens you're supposed to be taking care
of.

Rule 41

Definitely do not allow a Titanicite to smell your elbow.

Oooookay...

Rule 42

Luvpliian Warblers are always working an angle.
Do not agree to a deal.

Rule 43

Quiritixians have three clawed fingers; therefore,
it is considered rude to ask them to give you a high five.

Rule 44
If a Xxkyty child sheds their wings,
send them to bed without supper.

Rule 45
Never ask an alien family why they came to Earth.
It's considered poor etiquette.

Rule 46
A telepath's gem is the locus of their telekinetic abilities. To
put them in a telekinetic timeout, merely cover the gem with
a patch or headband.

Rule 47
When sitting for kids from Insomaru, limit their screen time to
1,439 Earthling minutes per day.

Rule 48
Always let a Vlorathian child beat you at poker.

Rule 49
Fluminian bedtime must be strictly adhered to.
Never let them stay up past 7:34 p.m.

Rule 50

Thoroughly read and carefully follow any supplementary special instructions left for you by the alien's parents.

Rule 51

Don't allow a child from Utivia to sleep in on Saturdays. Tuesdays are fine, of course.

Rule 52

Do not feed anything to an alien child that does not appear on the approved alien consumables list. Aliens' bodies cannot digest many Earthling ingredients.

Rule 53

Aliens from Tronolus don't have eyes.
They see with their toes. So always place their sunglasses on their feet and their shoes on their ears.

No way, that's awesome.

Rule 54

Don't catch an alien cold.

Rule 55

Also, don't catch an alien stomach virus, flu, or rash.

Rule 56
Especially don't catch an alien rash right
before class picture day. It won't be pretty.

Rule 57
Children from the Yupirian Belt must never break-dance.

Rule 58
Exposure to sizable crowds can overwhelm a telepath
with the thoughts and emotions of others, requiring the alien
to undergo emergency synaptic clearance protocol.
Keep them away from others.

Rule 59
Don't let an Octrothian child drink directly from the bathtub.

Rule 60
Aliens from Snarlon consider finger painting a sacred art.

Rule 61
When sitting for children from Gruto,
discipline obedience and reward misbehavior.

Rule 62

Don't sit on the baby. Seems clear; however,
we were unable to ascertain the origin of the human term
"babysitting." Perhaps you could enlighten us on its
Earthling etymology. *That sounds like a question for Olivia.*

Rule 63

An alien child must wear a helmet and kneepads while
riding a scooter, skateboard, or blender. If the alien has
two heads, two separate helmets are required.
If the alien has multiple knees or tentacle bends,
kneepads are required for all. *Blender riding? I gotta see that.*

Rule 64

Always brush your teeth before arriving to babysit. Aliens
have a keen sense of smell and are sensitive to the odor of
Homo sapiens' breath, particularly breath of the bad type. The
scent of soap, perfume, and taquitos is also unsavory.

Rule 65

Humans should avoid eating any alien candy, dessert,
or vegetables that contain the chemical known
as Gor-Monozine Neokine.

Rule 66

Do not attempt to bathe a Blurble. Blurbles have a violent
dislike of water and will quickly multiply and escape down
the drain.

Rule 67

Do not allow a kid from Korth to consume the raw fruit of a Klamalian tree. The exorbitant sugar content creates an unbearable behavioral instability.

Rule 68

Don't answer the door for strange aliens. Or strange humans. Or strange robots. But if it's a food delivery liaison dropping off a package of scrumptious Earthling pastries, be sure to sign for it forthwith. We practice stranger danger unless it involves dessert.

Rule 69

Never dress a Tyilian in jeans. Denim triggers their skin's hyper-sensory response system, which causes their scales to turn crusty.

Rule 70

An empath from Ehguzn can manipulate your emotions with ease. To prevent this occurrence, always wear a backward baseball cap in their presence.

Rule 71

Gor-Monites must have absolutely no soda pop of any sort. These aliens are digestive shape-shifters who transform into whatever they eat. If a Gor-Monite consumes soda, their body will absorb the volatile carbonated qualities of the drink, effectively turning them into a time bomb that will explode in approximately an hour, destroying them and anything within a hundred-yard radius. And as the babysitter, you will get to clean up the gooey mess that was once your ward.

Good times.

Rule 72

If a child hailing from the Pisxxir galaxy tells you a knock-knock joke of any sort, you must respond by saying "Flowers live on the floor." This secret password exchange establishes your identity as a friend. If you laugh or respond, "Who's there?" you are taken to be a foe.

Cool, cool . . .

Rule 73

Run any direct request for alien-sitting services by Principal Swift before accepting. He must be in the know at all times.

Rule 74

Never ask a kid from Vitreous Prime to control all the toilet water for your own personal gain.

Rule 75

To ensure body temperature stability,
feed a child from Bntuia one shoelace every hour.

Rule 76

Larqwans must apply moonscreen lotion
before heading outside at night.

Rule 77

Ligtorites are to consume no more than
three paper-napkin sandwiches a day.

Rule 78

Never ask a Gor-Monite to ingest your hair and shape-shift
into your clone for your own benefit. This includes scenarios
where the Gor-Monite clone takes a test for you, sits in
detention for you, or runs the mile in gym class for you. By
nature, Gor-Monites are legless blobs. They don't run. Ever.

FURTHER ALIEN TROUBLESHOOTING

So your Gor-Monite child is going to blow up

If you ignored rule seventy-one and permitted your Gor-Monite child to drink soda pop, the alien's stomach will begin to gurgle violently. You will have one hour to counteract the imminent carbonation combustion. To avoid explosion, feed the Gor-Monite child sodium silicate, a mineral found in the soil of Zzzansar VII, some polydimensional light beings, and Gor-Monite breath mints.

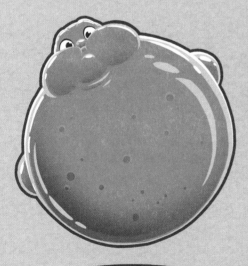

So your Gor-Monite child is rising

Your Gor-Monite ward ate dough while the yeast was still rising. Having assimilated the molecular structure of the active leavening agent, the child is converting fermentable sugars into carbon dioxide and ethanol, causing your Gor-Monite to expand at an alarming rate. To properly deflate your Gor-Monite, make a fist with your hand and push it gently into the puffy child. Continuously fold the edges of the child toward their stomach, one on top of the other, eventually forming a deflated Gor-Monite ball.

That's messed up, man. And yet, I kinda want to see it.

So your Blurbles have declared mutiny

Blurbles may appear to be harmless cutie-pies, but don't underestimate these charming fuzz balls. When mistreated, the self-multiplying beings grow hostile, rise up against their leader, and execute an aggressive coup with military precision—thus proving without a doubt that there is extra strength in numbers. To put an end to a Blurble rebellion, engage one of two available strategies. Either order your Orb to initiate eradication protocol and annihilate the Blurble population, or simply earn the trust of the Blurbles by putting their well-being before your own. We recommend you attempt the second option first.

So lemme ask, if you're sitting for a Blurble and they multiply, can you charge for extra kids or what?

How to stop Larqwan dust from turning your human skin green

To renew and regenerate their skin, Larqwans self-exfoliate. This cell shedding is a perfectly normal Larqwanian biological function. However, it is of the utmost importance that human skin not come in contact with the shed dust of a Larqwan. The emerald dust will turn your Earthling epidermis bright green. This condition will be permanent unless otherwise addressed. Please note: Larqwan dust is highly acidic. To counteract its tinting effects, apply any element with a lactose base, such as milk or yogurt, to *(Nacho cheese counts, right?)* the afflicted area. Doing so should turn an Earthling's green-tinted skin back to its regular shade.

At least one Duran sister read this tip, and it wasn't me. Nice going, Liv.

So your Snarlon cocooned themselves

Things have been awfully quiet upstairs. You knock on your Snarlon's bedroom door only to discover the child is missing and has been replaced by a cocoon. Every young Snarlon goes through a chrysalis phase, like the Earthling stage of puberty. Like Earthling teenage acne, cocooning is recurrent and often a source of embarrassment for the Snarlon. But smothering the cocoon in ranch dressing allows the issue to pass without scarring.

Ooooooooh. That explains the bottle of ranch in the medicine cabinet. But then, what's with the walnuts?

What to do when your Va'Taxian Vibra Bird is causing an earthquake

These avian aliens respond to the emotional vibrations of those around them. They become angry when you fight and calm when you make up. So the earthquake-ish tremors are merely birdspeak for "Can't we all just get along?" To put an end to the shakes, simply remain on amicable terms with those around you.

GABBY D'S TROUBLESHOOTING TIPS

Look at me. I've been babysitting aliens for a while now. And do I seem stressed out to you? Nah, cuz there's no such thing as a babysitting problem I can't handle. I am 100 percent pulling this thing off. So as long as we're talking troubleshooting, let me throw a few firsthand scenarios your way. Cuz Gaby D's in the house.

What to do when you're being held upside down by a Zagellian baby

Compared to your average human babysitting stuff, this is not normal. But it's just another day at the office for an alien sitter. The Zagellian is enjoying playtime. Just roll with it and enjoy the upside-down view. A new perspective never hurt anyone.

How to NOT get edged out by another babysitter

I'll admit, I felt threatened or jealous or whatever when Olivia chose Susie over me. And maybe I got a little carried away with the whole alien candy revenge plot. Okay, I get that, I guess. But, hey, it all worked out fine, just like I knew it would. In the end it came down to doing what I do best: being the sitter with the style that makes the kiddies go wild. And in this case, that kiddie was Olivia. And even a super-sitter like Susie can't compete with the Duran sisters' bond.

So your bud day party got out of control

I threw Jeremy a bud day party, which was lit until it wasn't.
A random alien started melting Liv's trophies, and one of
Timbuk's friends started sniffing my mom's potatoes. Why
would anyone even do that? The party got out of hand, like
way out of hand. So I went full mom. I put on a painful party
animal T-shirt, did some '90s dance moves, the whole deal.
But you know what? Kids couldn't leave that party fast
enough. No one commits a party foul like Gabby D. Huh, that
sounded way cooler in my head.

I got the coolest DJ
in the galaxy to spin
tunes at Jeremy's
bud day party.

Your Gor-Monite child won't floss their teeth

Gor-Monites have like a bazillion rows of teeth that they're
  supposed to brush and floss while in blob form. If your
Gor-Monite kid's anything like Jeremy, they won't be down
  with it. Try busting out this trick: Replace standard floss
with a twelve-foot bungee cord. Stretch the cord across
  the room, securing each end to a heavy bookcase, dresser,
or whatever's right there. Have the blob slide back and forth
across the room, with the bungee between their teeth. For
an extra challenge, set the timer on your phone and see how
fast they floss their whole mouth.

How to get gum out of alien fur

No one told me not to feed bubble gum to a Blurble.
But since a similar thing once happened to me while
  babysitting Liv, I knew what to do. Slather the sticky
fur in mayonnaise or creamy peanut butter. Work it
  through the fur and gum with your fingers.
Wait ten minutes for it to work. The gum should
  become stiffer and slide right off the fur.
  Who's a babysitting genius? I am.

THE
UNSITTABLES
DOSSIER

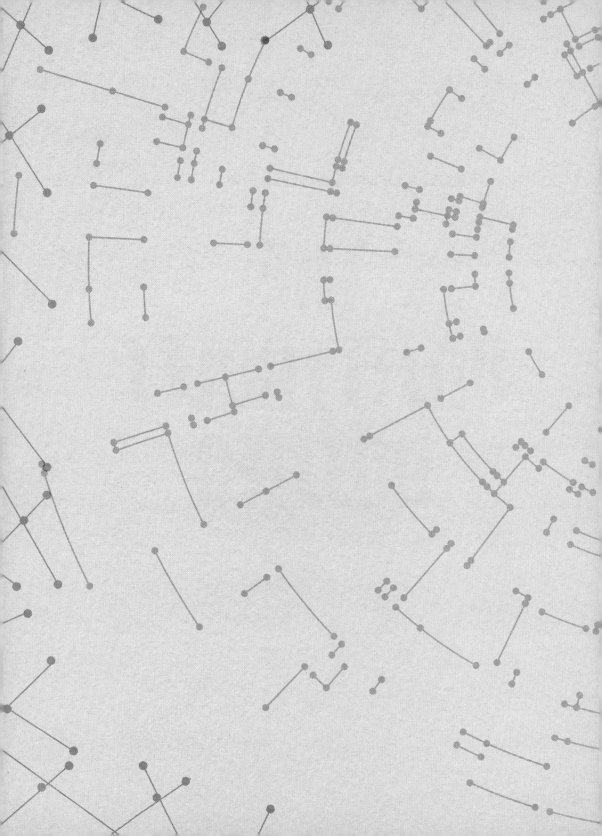

All right, Gabby. Now that I've selected you for the prestigious honor of babysitting the aliens of Havensburg, I shall reveal to you a reference guide of potential clients. This file does not in any way represent the totality of the Havensburg alien population but rather a subset of several key alien children you may find yourself in the presence of. Think of this as your client cheat sheet, if you will.

These children, of course, are quite vulnerable and will be susceptible to your influence. I am counting on you, Gabby, to carry on with highest character and the utmost respect.

It is by no accident that I have chosen you to be our sitter. I see something very special in you, Gabby: a spark that is not easily extinguished. I believe you have the makings of an inimitable babysitter and an irreplaceable friend.

Thank you in advance for all your help and hard work. My appreciation knows no bounds.

As all the hip Earthlings say, "later, gator."

PRINCIPAL PRINCIPAL SWIFT

Principal Principal Swift

Name: Jeremy

Age: 8

Species: Gor-Monite

Jeremy hates when anyone calls him by his proper Gor-monite name, Franis. But I'm not afraid to pull that puppy out when he's acting all stubborn and annoying and, well, like a total Franis.

Unique physical traits: Six feet tall, green, blob-like, with seven rows of extremely sharp teeth

Talents and abilities: Gor-Monites are digestive shape-shifters who assimilate the molecular structure of anything they digest, thus taking on the physical form of whatever they eat.

Favorite thing about living on Earth: Nachos

Special parental instructions: Jeremy is heir to the Gor-Monite throne. There are some Gor-Monites who do not wish to see him ascend as supreme leader. The babysitter must be sure to keep Jeremy safe at all times, no matter what.

Please know that at times, Jeremy's attitude is less than stellar. He does not think he needs a sitter, which is precisely why he does need one.

Babysitter's Notes:

Jeremy is awesome. Or as Jeremy would say, "baller." I love babysitting him. He'll always be my first alien. Yeah, he can be difficult to watch sometimes, but can you blame him?

The poor blob is cooped up inside all day with just the Orb for company. No bowling, no mini golf, no drive-throughs. Which is why it's my personal responsibility to see he has fun after school.

Jeremy as a human

Jeremy in blob form

I plan all kinds of cool activities for us to do together. You know, typical babysitting stuff, like transforming into a condor, getting kidnapped by Blorgs, and nearly exploding from soda pop. Good times, good times . . .

Name: Sky

Age: 13

Species: Telepath

Unique physical traits: Small lights on her bald head

Talents and abilities: Touch telepathy

Favorite thing about living on Earth: Earthling teen culture, Sir Francis Drake

Special parental instructions: Her neural pathways align with anyone she touches, allowing her to download their thoughts and emotions into her brain. So do not allow her to touch any humans.

Babysitter's Notes:

Sky is 13. She's way too old for a babysitter. But she's the perfect age to be my friend. Yes, I have a legit outer-space alien for a friend. Pretty dope.

Name: Kali

Age: 8

Species: Gwargwar

Unique physical traits: Blue skin covered with tribal tattoos

Talents and abilities: Throwing spears, shooting darts, firing slingshots, and removing fingers

Favorite thing about living on Earth: Being the fiercest warrior on this wimpy planet

Special parental instructions: Kali hails from a war-ridden, savage world and tends to be intense. She's quick to fight. Do not upset her.

Babysitter's Notes:

Kali is one tough kid, but I can handle her. She frowns on anything she views as weak, like comfortable couches, participation trophies, and taquito breaks. She's fiercely loyal and protective, which is awesome. And she taught me to face my fears head-on. But that girl needs to loosen up. Good thing I'm an expert at chilling. I mean, how hard can it be to teach a Gwargwar to relax?

Name: Timbuk

Age: 9

Species: Stylus

Unique physical traits: Super-deep voice, small elephant-like trunk for a nose

Talents and abilities: Writes a popular style blog; also excels at playing Punchy Arm

Favorite thing about living on Earth: Fashion, parties

Special parental instructions: Timbuk tends to think he's the coolest alien in the room. Do not stroke his ego.

Babysitter's Notes:

Word of advice: do not invite Timbuk to a party you're not supposed to be throwing in the first place. Timbuk and his fashion blog followers can get out of control pretty quickly. Also, how does that kid have a fashion blog? All he wears is black.

Name: Stewart Fischman

Age: 9

Species: Vitreous Prime

Unique physical traits: The Fischmans belong to a species of underwater dwellers. As such, young Stewart breathes through gills located on his neck. He also sports a prominent fin on his head. Fish boy Stewart's Mohawk fin is the bomb.

Talents and abilities: Stewart is hydrokinetic. He can manipulate and control water with his mind, juggling it, moving it, and even shaping it into huge free-floating bubbles large enough for him to swim in.
^(and pee)

Favorite thing about living on Earth: Nothing. Stewart doesn't trust humans, because they pollute Earth's oceans and turn their fish into sticks.

Special parental instructions: Stewart sleeps in a large aquatic water tank. When he is ready to go to sleep, be sure to fill the tank all the way up to the line with water. This bedtime gesture is the Vitreous Prime equivalent of tucking in your child.

Babysitter's Notes:

Watching Stewart is cool. He's a good kid. Sure, he gets super skittish around Earthlings, but after hanging with me and Wesley, he's starting to warm up to the idea of humans. I definitely get it. I mean, it took me a while to warm up to the idea of living in Havensburg, and I only moved eight states away. That kid moved like eight galaxies.

Witnessing an alien birth was at the top of Wesley's bucket list, so I let him name this baby Va'Taxian Vibra Bird Wesley Jr.

Name: Wesley Jr.

Age: Newborn

Species: Va'Taxian Vibra Bird

Unique physical traits: Birdlike feathers

Talents and abilities: Emits strong vibrational energy when he gets upset; possesses an accelerated speed of growth

Favorite thing about living on Earth: Watching happy humans

Special parental instructions: Keep the egg under the warming light and watch it while the owners are on vacation. The egg will not hatch until the owners are back. If it does hatch, please remain happy around the bird at all times. It responds to the emotional vibrations of those around it. If you're angry, the bird gets upset. If you're relaxed, the bird grows calm.

Babysitter's Notes:

Can I just say, that egg cracked three hours after I started watching it, and out popped an alien earthquake bird. I should have read the instructions. Would have saved me and Wesley a lot of time and trouble and stopped a lot of buildings from shaking.

Also, I know we made up and all, but I really hate when Wesley and I fight.

Name: Fritz

Age: 7

Species: Pantera

Unique physical traits: Tiny gremlin-like alien who controls a humanlike android body. Furry alien Fritz has four antennae, three fingers, and three toes and comes in hot at four inches tall. Since alien Fritz builds android Fritz, android Fritz's looks are varied.

Talents and abilities: Engineering genius who makes his own robot bodies

Favorite thing about living on Earth: Girls

Special parental instructions: Don't be fooled by his cute, furry appearance. He can build androids and all sorts of other robotic gadgets.

Babysitter's Notes:
Fritz is the sweetest. But sometimes kids develop innocent crushes on their babysitters. If this happens, ya gotta let them down easy. Let the kid know you think he's special, but as a friend. And that someday he'll meet a gremlin-slash-android his own age who will be crushing all over him. There are no broken hearts in babysitting.

Name: Pip

Age: 6

Species: Praxian Fairy

Unique physical traits: Tiny alien fairy-insect with wings; may leave behind a trail of glittery fairy goop

Talents and abilities: Flying through small spaces; sneaking into backpacks and purses

Favorite thing about living on Earth: Surprising humans with fairy flybys.

Special parental instructions: Praxian Fairies are not dangerous, just very, very naughty. Be prepared for mischief-making.

Babysitter's Notes:

Here's the deal: Praxian Fairies are not well-behaved. I'd throw them in the category of troublemakers. Being a troublemaker myself sometimes, I know how to handle them.

Just swat 'em into a dishwasher or suck 'em up with a vacuum until they agree to cooperate. Think of it as putting them in a creative time-out.

Name: Zak

Age: Infant

Species: Zagellian

Unique physical traits: Flailing purple tentacles

Talents and abilities: Each of a baby Zagellian's tentacles is strong enough to lift a human upside down into the air.

Favorite thing about living on Earth: Tickling humans

Special parental instructions: A Zagellian's ear is often mistaken for their mouth hole. Take precautions not to deliver food into the wrong receptacle.

Babysitter's Notes:

When a Zagellian says, "Feed me," you need to comply. Right away.

Zagellians have so many tentacles! You have to keep track of where they are at all times.

Name: Lars

Age: 3

Species: Larqwan

Unique physical traits: Glittering green skin that sheds, leaving a trail of green dust that stains

Talents and abilities: Larqwans like to cuddle. Be warned. One hug quickly becomes a sparkly green mess.

Favorite thing about living on Earth: Saint Patrick's Day

Special parental instructions: Larqwans shed brilliant shimmering green dust that can turn humans green.

Babysitter's Notes:

Guess I should have read that bit about shedding before I babysat a Larqwan. Good thing Olivia did! Mom's glittering green skin would not have looked good on camera.
Or on those weird Channel 6 mugs she's always trying to give away.

Name: Buddy

Age: 13

Species: Blorg

Unique physical traits: Cranial cybertronic implants, pale skin, and silver hair

Talents and abilities: Rave-dancing to Blorgian psycho-pop

Favorite thing about living on Earth: Techno music and causing trouble

Special parental instructions: Blorgs like to travel in packs, so to avoid trouble, try to limit contact with other Blorgs.

Babysitter's Notes:

Gotta say, they're not my fav. They definitely think they're too swag for tag. If I had to choose between spending an afternoon with a Blorg and dealing with my dirty restaurant toilet phone, it'd be a toss-up.

Name: Daria Mungo

Age: 10

Species: Mungo

Unique physical traits: Slender, humanoid aliens with paper-thin skin, they all wear glasses to expand their visual capabilities while sewing. Their teeth are sharp and yellowed, and their eyes are sunken and cloudy, with dark circles around them.

Talents and abilities: Sewing and tailoring

Favorite thing about living on Earth: Humans come in so many different textures.

Special parental instructions: Do not enter any areas of the house without first receiving permission.

Babysitter's Notes:

When babysitting a Mungo, be sure to hold on to your skin—literally. They like to make suits out of unusual materials. Or at least the Mungo family did before they ended up in alien prison. So BYOF—bring your own fabric. Also, your own snacks. They have exactly zero good snacks in their fridge.

Name: Jeremy (II)

Age: Unknown

Species: Blurble

Unique physical traits: Adorable fluffy little ball of purple alien cuteness

Talents and abilities: Can divide and multiply, turning into a large Blurble squadron

Favorite thing about living on Earth: Causing chaos among humans

Special parental instructions: Blurbles are much more formidable than they appear. Many a would-be ruler has been driven mad by their wily ways. They're known to distract their victims while collecting parts to assemble into weapons—for example, a giant crossbow.

Babysitter's Notes:

Gor-Monite Jeremy told me how Blurble Jeremy transformed into dozens of Blurbles and declared mutiny on him. Obviously, if I had been there, none of that would have happened, as I am the most responsible babysitter I know and nothing crazy ever happens on my watch. Well, maybe there have been just a few moments of chaos, but nothing earthshaking. Actually, that's not true. The entire Earth did shake once. But that was so not my fault. I blame the Va'Taxian Vibra Bird.

Before the mutiny

Name: Jonas

Age: Unknown

Species: Zaroodan Invisi-lizard

Unique physical traits: A chubby dragon lizard—like creature with six arms, eight eyes, and a forked tail

Talents and abilities: Advanced cloaking mechanism

Special parental instructions: Owned by Jimbuk, cousin of Timbuk. He says no special instructions come to mind.

Babysitter's Notes:

Keep this lizard away from warm, thick, saucy substances, like, say, I don't know . . . a large vat of steaming carnitas. It's where they like to lay their eggs. Also maybe give the sitter a heads-up if they're watching a pregnant pet. Is that too much to ask?

Name: Jimbuk

Age: 11

Species: Stylus

Unique physical traits: Super-deep voice, piglike snout

Talents and abilities: Junior Olympic Punchy Arm runner-up

Favorite thing about living on Earth: Enjoys hanging out with his first cousin, Timbuk

Special parental instructions: Like his cousin, Jimbuk tends to make his own rules. Keep him reined in before things get out of control.

Babysitter's Notes:

This kid enjoys ingesting, then barfing up invisible lizard babies. Way to be extra creepy, kid.

Name: Dranis

Age: 8

Species: Gor-Monite

Unique physical traits: Six-foot greenish-blue blob with rows and rows of extremely sharp teeth

Talents and abilities: Masterminding the destruction of Havensburg

Favorite thing about living on Earth: Has never been to Earth but wants to blow it up

Special parental instructions: As the direct spawnling of the supreme leader, Dranis called "not it" to following in her dad's footsteps. Therefore, the responsibility fell to her brother, Franis (aka Jeremy).

Babysitter's Notes:

Dranis isn't evil, she just misses her bro. I get that. I don't know what I'd do if Olivia moved away from me. I might not threaten to blow up a town—that's a little nutso—but I'd definitely go after her. Not exactly looking forward to watching her and Jeremy together when she visits Havensburg. I'm definitely charging Swifty more for that.

INTERGALACTIC GIZMOS, GADGETS, AND SECRET ROOMS

PROCEED WITH CAUTION!

Such is the nature of watching intergalactic unsittables that you may accidentally come into unsanctioned contact with an intergalactic gadget.

But unless given specific permission by the client, do not touch, point, push, squeeze, flick, throw, hug, or eat the alien device. That last part about not consuming the gadget should be obvious, but if you're babysitting Gor-Monites, everything but the furniture is a potential snack. Scratch that; even the furniture is a potential snack. The little blobkins find it hilarious to morph into couch cushions, brooms, and the wayward remote control.

As such, on the following pages are some of the alien tools you may encounter and absolutely will not use.

Accidentally? If you're babysitting aliens, there's no way you just accidentally happen to come across their space gadgets. C'mon, it's pretty much a given that a babysitter's going to case the place. I mean, it's practically a babysitter's right to rummage through a client's stuff. Especially in an alien's house—those homes are begging to be searched. In fact, some might say it would be rude not to snoop around. Am I right?

Gadget: Orb

Planet of origin: Gor-Monia

Owner: Principal Principal Swift

Function: Part teacher, part intergalactic doctor, part curmudgeonly butler, the multifaceted Orb can do it all: scan brain functions, perform thought transfers, carry out complex medical procedures, and tutor Jeremy. And the Orb manages to do it all with a very poor attitude.

Constructed like an all-in-one tool, the Orb's built-in laser-tipped appendages include a scalpel, a needle, a razor, a pincher, and a laser cannon.

As the educator to the future supreme leader of Gor-Monia, the Orb is in possession of an encyclopedic amount of knowledge about the planet and its culture. If only young Jeremy would listen to the Orb. The two tend to have a vitriolic relationship and don't exactly get along.

Caution: Though Jeremy often dismisses the Orb as a mere device, do not underestimate its intelligence. The Orb is underwhelmed by its duties and does not appreciate being disrespected. As the Orb often says, "My revenge will be delicious."

Babysitter's notes:

First time I met the Orb, it threatened to probe me. So naturally, I bicycle-kicked it across the room. But now Orbie and I are super close. That shiny soccer ball of a robot has helped me out of some major babysitting jams. I've got mad respect for the sphere.

Gadget: Flip-phone controller

Planet of origin: Gor-Monia

Owner: Principal Principal Swift

Function: This incredibly powerful piece of alien technology will aid you in your babysitting duties. I have disguised this interstellar tech in the form of Earth's most cutting-edge technology: the flip phone. I also considered the Walkman and the eight-track player, but no one uses those anymore. Plus, I find the action of repeatedly flipping the phone open and shut in the human palm to be quite enjoyable.

Yo, Swifty, my abuela called.
She wants her old-timey phone back.

The flip-phone device is multifunctional, with a complex Gor-Monite interface. Please carefully read these detailed directions before use:

- If you are in peril and want to emit a ray of energy that will disintegrate everything in its path, press the ꜰ button.

- If you are in danger and want to emit a gamma-ray pulse that temporarily paralyzes a being and causes them to pass out, press the ꝛ button.

- If you are lost and want to see a rotating 3-D hologram of your current location, press the ꝉ button.

- If the child you're babysitting won't stop crying and you'd like to mute them, press the ꝥ button.

- If you'd like to order a pizza, use your own personal phone and dial Havensburg 'Za. They deliver.

- Should you be loaned an official alien flip phone for a specific sitting venture, you must return it at the end of your shift.

Babysitter's notes:

If Swifty was hoping to design something that blended in seamlessly with Earth culture, he failed. By about two decades. Which is why I never use it. I tried it a few times, but it's just not my jam. (Sorry about disintegrating your vase.) If there's a real babysitting emergency, it's much easier to kick down a door.

Gadget: Underground comms room

Planet of origin: Gor-Monia

Owner: Principal Principal Swift

Function: This all-in-one high-tech command console connects Earth to Gor-Monite life. Its abilities are infinite.

Hidden away in a secret panel behind the wall of an otherwise boring suburban basement, this black-and-white room houses a high-tech communication console. This Earthling escritoire houses a computer that translates reports into Gor-Monite glyphs and delivers them to Glor-Bron and the Gor-Monite Central Archive. These reports cover such critical cultural observations as a comparative study of the Hemsworth brothers' handsomeness, an academic analysis of the word "booyah," and a thesis on the art of getting paid to listen to street jazz.

Olivia explained that's just a fancy crossword-puzzle word for "desk." Who knew?

The communications hub computer is further programmed with an interactive holographic map of the universe, a planet-destruction simulator, and the ability to stream prime-time Gor-Monian television series like *The Real Blob-Wives of Gor-Monia*, the delectably overdramatic soap opera *Gor-Monite Nights*, and the very bingeable *Project Blobway*. Make it work, blobs.

Babysitter's notes:

When I first woke up in this room, I was strapped to a chair.

<u>Not cool.</u> But now I kinda think of it as our own dope alien clubhouse.

Gadget: Mind-wipe box

Planet of origin: Gor-Monia

Owner: Principal Principal Swift

Function: This small silver cube with a single button on top can wipe minds clean, particularly the minds of humans who possess knowledge about alien existence and shouldn't. Once engaged, the cube eliminates all memories of alien presence on Earth, along with any memories the human has of friends, family, and the good old days. It's basically a reset button for the brain.

Just kidding. Gor-Monites don't have mind-wiping technology. It's just a normal box where I store an interesting-rock collection and one random tooth.

Babysitter's notes:

Gotta hand it to Swifty, he totally had me and Wesley fooled with his mind-wipe bluff. I did not know he had that prank in him. He's really starting to get the hang of Earthling culture after all.

Gadget: Ancient Hammer of Gwargwar

Planet of origin: Gwar Gwar

Owner: Mr. and Mrs. Kali's Parents

Function: Forged eons ago by the rebel chieftain Gkwartin the First, this battle-worn hammer was wielded by many a heroic leader in the fight for Gwargwarian independence. Passed down through the generations, it now serves to protect Kali as she looks to survive on the mean streets of Havensburg.

Babysitter's notes:

Probably not the time, but hey, I'm gonna go for it. I'm not exactly sure that you need the Ancient Hammer to survive on the mean streets of Havensburg. The most dangerous thing in town is the beans at Luchachos. So Kali might be able to cool it with the pummeling and hammer swinging. Just a thought.

Gadget: Blorg mind wipe

Planet of origin: Blorg

Owner: Jeremy (who stole it from some Blorg teenagers, who stole it from their parents)

Function: This device can be programmed to erase all memories formed during a precise set of time coordinates. With a quick white flash, any knowledge collected during the designated time phase will cease to exist.

Caution: This device is glitchy and may cause side effects.

Babysitter's notes:

Glitchy? How about broken? That stupid mind-wipe thing doesn't even work. Rather than erase our memories of the four hours before we used the device, like it was supposed to, that weird box erased our memories of the four hours after we used it. So that happened? Honestly, you Blorgs can keep your janky tech.

Gadget: Tailorfile

Planet of origin: Mungo

Owner: Mungo family

Function: When activated, the device projects a holographic calendar, date, and address book. It also captures design sketches, client measurements, fabric inventory, and the company ledger.

Caution: Mungos are private beings known to go to extreme measures to keep their secrets, um . . . secret.

Babysitter's notes:

I found this hidden directory where the Mungos stored their mastermind blueprints. Their evil alien tailor plot? I shut that down real quick. I love the fact that I just wrote "evil alien tailor plot." Proof that my life in Havensburg is not boring.

Gadget: Detention circle

Planet of origin: Mungo

Owner: Mungo family

Function: An imprisoning circular force field that uses waist- and neck-high emitters to halt movement and neutralize any effort to escape or shape-shift.

Caution: Any Gor-Monite imprisoned by a detention circle will lose the ability to take a form besides resting blob shape.

Babysitter's notes:

Oh yeah, I called it. I was right. Those unsmiling tailors were up to no good. Score one for Gabby D.

Also, while saving Swifty, I got to wield the Ancient Hammer of Gwargwar. I take back what I said earlier. In Havensburg, you definitely need a shockwave-emitting mallet to make it through the day.

Gadget: Interplanetary invite

Planet of origin: Paradizio

Owner: Dranis

Turns out, there's no such planet. It's from Gor-Monia, where else. . . .

Function: This DNA-activated handheld device sports two finger scanners that reveal a hidden scroll screen. The device can transmit images, voice-over, and holographic videos.

Babysitter's notes:

In my defense, I didn't go snooping around to find this device. It came to me. In the mail. How was I supposed to know it was a trap? It smelled like taquitos and sunshine!

Gadget: Space-travel suit

Planet of origin: Paradizio _Not_ a real planet!

Owner: Gabby Duran

Function: Coming in at one inch tall, this one-size-fits-all space suit automatically adjusts to the size of its wearer.

Babysitter's notes:

Not gonna find this look at the Havensburg mall. Still, the suit wasn't all that. We're talking about my outer space debut. I had to put my own signature spin on it.

Gadget: Flying space lounge

Planet of origin: Multiple

It's the Hummer stretch limo of outer space travel. I only arrive in style, baby.

Function: Looking to travel first-class through space? This intergalactic transport system features red velvet booths, a chilled dessert dispenser, and a DJ spinning cosmic tunes. That's what we Gor-Monites call traveling in style.

Babysitter's notes:

I regret falling for Dranis's dumb trick. I do not regret traveling to outer space. As Jeremy would say, it was baller.

ONE LAST THING:
GOOD LUCK, EARTHLING!

When we first moved to Havensburg, I thought it was a giant snore. But who knew it was actually a hotbed of alien activity? And I get to babysit alien kids from all over the galaxy—from fierce warriors and fish kids to gremlins who operate androids and, of course, shape-shifters, like Jeremy. I have the coolest job in the galaxy!